Escape

By

Nate Johnson

Purple Herb Publishing

AuthorNateJo@gmail.com

https://www.facebook.com/AuthorNateJo/

Dedicated to

Keith Snodgrass

Other books by Nate Johnson

Escape

Chapter One

Haley

Oh, how I wish I could be that bored again. I honestly think it is the last time in my life I will ever feel that carefree sense of nothing to do. No emergency to be dealt with, no drama. Just a lazy Saturday morning on spring break.

I was lying on my bed, my hands behind my head staring up at the ceiling wondering where my friends were and what they were doing. Maybe just a bit sad. They had homes, families, adventures.

I know, wah wah wah. But at the time I was a seventeen-year-old girl, alone in the dormitory, with nothing to do. It is in our nature to worry that we're missing out.

My family had sort of disintegrated earlier that year. Uncle Frank had received an offer to teach in Seattle. Which meant moving from Tulsa Oklahoma to the Pacific Northwest. My older brother Chase had taken off. Saying he wanted to see the world. But I knew he was just running from the anger that burned his soul.

I'd decided I was going to use my parent's life insurance money to go to an artsy boarding high school in New York City for my senior year.

"It's the best way to get into Columbia," I'd told my Uncle. "And I'll be eighteen in six months. I'll just do it anyway."

My cousins Ryan and Cassie had sided with me. They knew this was my dream. And a girl has to reach for her dream or live a life of regret.

Uncle Frank had lost before he even started fighting. But I loved him for it. He'd raised the four of us, Ryan, Cassie, Chase, and me ever since my parents and his wife had been killed by a drunk driver five years ago. - May he rot in hell -. A memory that still rips at my heart at least once or twice a day.

I'd been with them over Christmas, in Seattle. Only Chase's absence was a sore point that made the holidays feel empty. But I'd come back to school, stoked to finish out the year while I waited for acceptance to Columbia.

All that changed with a simple phone call.

"Uncle Frank?" I answered, ecstatic to have something interrupting the monotony of life.

"Blue Jester," he said, making my stomach clench. Our family's secret code. This was serious. Deadly type serious.

I paused as my mind tried to take it in.

"Are you there Haley?" he asked. The tone of his voice along with the secret code set off warning signals.

"Yes," I managed to say as I held my breath, waiting.

"It's going to hit," he said, "The asteroid. You need to get out of the city."

"What? Huh?""

"Listen," he said firmly. "They made a mistake, the asteroid is going to hit us. It's not going to miss us like they thought. I think in the Pacific but I'm not sure. We're still working the numbers."

I fumbled to understand as a thousand thoughts and questions raced through my brain. None of this made sense. I'd seen the news. I wasn't an oblivious troglodyte. We'd even discussed it just before my friends took off. Sheryl joked that if the asteroid hit us, she wouldn't have to take the history test next week.

But this didn't make sense. Of course, that thought was followed by a sick certainty. My uncle was not the kind of person to get something like this wrong. A scientist. He was rock solid. The salt of the earth type. He'd taken on raising four teenagers and done a great job. I loved him for it. But this?

"I've already called Ryan," he said. "He's headed for Papa's farm in Idaho. You need to get out of New York. Even if it hits the Pacific, the wave will work its way around and reach New York. If it hits in the Atlantic..." there was a long pause. "If it hits in the Atlantic, ... I don't know."

Suddenly, a wave of fear flashed through me. I'd gone from confusion to terror in an instant.

"But," he continued, "I'm like ninety-nine percent sure it will hit in the Pacific,"

Still, I fumbled around in my brain as I tried to understand.

Taking a deep breath he said, "Listen, I don't have time, I've got to call Chase and Cassie. Just get out. The city will become a mad house."

My stomach clenched as I thought about how bad it could be. The city lived on the edge. One of the many reasons I loved it. Something like this. ... I don't know. It was impossible to think what would happen.

"Get to Papa's if you can," he said with a heavy sigh.

I barked out a laugh, "Idaho? That's on the other side of the country. Will there be flights? How do I get from Spokane to the farm? Will someone come get me?"

"There might be an EMP. No flying. You might have to walk."

"What?" No this was impossible. Like I said, my uncle was a scientist. An astrophysicist. One of those guys who knew stuff. And he was never wrong. A good thing in an uncle. "I can't walk to Idaho."

"You have to," he said, and I could hear the sadness in his voice. "Get away from cities, get out into the country."

I was still trying to take it all in when he said, "I've got to call Cassie and Chase. Are you going to be all right?"

"Ha," I snapped. I'd just been informed that the world was going to end. I was alone, on the other side of the country. Alone, and terrified. And oh yeah, civilization was going to be ripped away.

"Listen, Haley," he said. "I love you. I am proud of you. Your Mom and Dad would be so proud of the woman you have become. Always remember that. You are loved and the safest place for you is your grandfather's farm."

My heart melted, he sounded like he was saying goodbye. Not just now, but forever. Suddenly I realized what he was saying, he didn't expect to live through this. My heart broke. Once again, I was losing someone I loved. Someone I needed.

"You have to get away," I said to him. "We need you."

"I've got to go," he said with a sadness that tore at me. "I love you."

Then there was the loudest click, and I knew I'd lost my uncle.

A cold fear filled me as I tried to pull myself together. The world was going to end. There was never any doubt in my mind. You had to know my uncle to understand why I was so sure. If he said so, then it was true.

Get out of the city, he said. I laughed. A nervous laugh full of terror. I was on the east coast. It was one big city for hundreds of miles. How? Even if I had a car I didn't know how to drive. A plane? He said no planes. But how else?

"Get out," I growled to myself as I realized I was procrastinating, one of my faults. Something I was working on. This was not the time to dawdle, I realized as fear filled me. I needed to act, not sit, and think about it for the next two days.

Swinging my feet over the edge of my bed, I froze. Act? How? Do what? What if I did the wrong thing and made everything worse? Or did something useless and miss something important?

A thousand thoughts tumbled through my brain as I tried to sort it all out. "Just go," I cursed myself as I grabbed a bookbag and started stuffing it with things. I was zipping it shut when I realized I was being stupid and dumped it all out on my bed and started repacking. This time focusing on being smart, not fast. Jeans, T-shirts, a fleece Pendleton, girl stuff, extra socks, and underwear. I'd wear my gray pea coat. It'd be warm, but I might need it.

I grabbed my purse and pulled out my wallet, opening I made sure both the debit card and my emergency credit card were there and counted forty-three dollars in bills. I'd have to hit an ATM and a supermarket. But I needed to get out of the city first.

I quickly changed out of tennis shoes to hiking boots. Smiling, I shook my head. Cassie bought them for me last Christmas. I preferred them to cowboy boots when we went riding at Papa's farm.

God, was she okay? A new fear filled me. Cassie was the youngest. And she was in Oklahoma for the week. Right now, her father was telling her the world was going to end. How was she handling it? Like an expert, I thought with a smile. Nothing phased Cassie.

Once I slung my pack over my shoulder I turned and examined our room, wondering what I had forgotten. Then I thought of Sheryl's chocolate stash.

"Sorry," I said as I opened the bottom drawer of her dresser and pulled back the sweaters to find six large candy bars. Hersey Milk Chocolate. I didn't hesitate, she'd understand. And I'd pay her back.

Suddenly I realized I might never see her again. I might never see anyone I knew ever again. An empty hollowness filled me as I was finally beginning to understand just what was happening.

12

Pushing the fear and sorrow down deep, I hurried out of the room, down the hall, and flew down the stairs to the school's front door. And froze. The world seemed too normal. High blue spring sky, the normal city smells, oil, cement, and sour garbage. The normal sounds of cars, a subway rumbling underground, people going about their business. Just another day in the city.

Twisting, I headed north. The George Washington bridge. It was the obvious choice, head west. Eight miles away. How long do I have? Uncle Frank hadn't said, but he sounded so nervous, it had to be soon. I'd be dark before I made the bridge.

"The subway," I mumbled to myself as I darted across the street to the station. As I hurried down the steps I tried to calm my racing heart. The world was about to change forever. How? I mean, what did it mean? Was this a dinosaur killer type? Less, more? If it hit the Pacific, how could the wave get here?

These and a thousand other questions raced through my mind as I swiped my subway card and headed for the "A" platform. The place was semi-deserted. Or as deserted as New York gets.

"Saturday morning," I said to myself.

An older woman gave me a quick look then backed off three steps. New Yorkers avoid people who talk to themselves.

I gave her a quick smile then wondered if I should tell her that an asteroid was going to hit the earth and she should get away. No, she'd know I was crazy then. No one would believe me. Sadness filled me. There was nothing I could do to help anyone. I just had to get out.

Scoffing to myself, I shook my head, Papa's farm. Impossible.

The older woman took another two steps away then moved down the platform determining to get in a different car.

"Come on," I said as I pulled out my phone and checked the time. The train was taking forever. They came every six minutes. Should I abandon this and try for a cab? I had just turned to leave when I felt that rumble under my feet followed by the rush of air of an approaching train.

Letting out a deep breath I forced myself to remain calm. I couldn't hurry things. I had to be patient.

When the doors opened, I checked inside real quick. A common practice. I always made sure there were no obvious crazies or creeps. If there were, I'd move down a couple of cars. This was pretty clear. A dozen people, couples, workmen returning from a long shift. A college girl at the far end.

I hurried in and got a seat on the far side. Closing my eyes I began trying to develop a plan and came up completely short. How could I plan? I had no idea what was going to happen.

The train rocked as it took off, making me let out a long sigh. I was going, the first step in a long journey, making progress. Only about three thousand more miles to go.

We hit two more stops, frustrating me to no end, making me wait and grind my teeth. Then we were off again as I tried to calm myself.

Suddenly, the lights flickered then went out as the train lurched and began to slow.

An old man cursed.

My stomach fell as I fought to stop from screaming. First off, I hate the dark. And I needed to get out. The stupid Transit System choosing this moment to screw up was not conducive to my mental health.

A weak light at the end of the subway car gave just enough light to show the frightened faces as people looked around trying to figure out what was happening. That was when it hit me with full force. This wasn't the subway screwing up. This was the world ending.

Chapter Two

Tanner

You know things are going bad when airplanes start falling out of the sky. I stood there with my jaw dropping as a big jet turned turtle and nosed dove into the Hudson. Not like Sully landing safely, I mean, straight in.

At the same time, a yellow cab crashed into the back of a limo.

I was still trying to figure it all out when the silence hit me. That empty silence that was so weird. I mean, New York isn't ever quiet. But this was just eerie. No cars, no window air conditioners, no distant sirens. Nothing. Even the plane crash had been quiet.

A cold shiver shot down my spine as I twisted to try and take it all in. Listen, one thing I'd learned early growing up in Hell's Kitchen. Keep your head on a swivel. Know who and what was going on. Sometimes it was the only way a person survived.

Sure, things might have been different this last year. I was a big guy. Real big. And I didn't have to worry much, but old habits die hard. This was all just too weird.

Then the second jet swooped overhead, clipped its wing, and tumbled into a downtown skyscraper.

September Eleven? Were we under attack? I'd grown up on stories about that day. Was it happening again? But the cars? And the stop lights were out. Had they hit the power grid at the same time they took over the planes. Or had they flown a plan into the powerplant? But again, every car had stopped working.

An anger began to build inside of me. I'd tear them apart. How dare they hurt my city. And yes, I hated New York. But I was allowed to. I lived there.

People were pulling out cell phones then frowning, obviously coming up empty. I scoffed and shook my head. One thing about being poor. I didn't have to worry about a cell signal.

A middle-aged woman stepped out of her cab, lifting her cell phone trying to get a signal. She had lawyer written all over her. High-end business suit, expensive briefcase. And a downtown lawyer, not a legal aid lawyer. And yes, I can tell the difference. I'd had some experience with the legal aid types.

I stepped off the curb to ask her if she knew what was going on. Her face registered surprise then fear as she gripped her briefcase and stepped back.

My gut tightened. I'd seen that look a lot lately. People just naturally freaked around me. I'd just turned eighteen and was six-four and two forty of solid muscle. Black hair, gray eyes, a scar on my chin. But I think they saw something

17

in my eyes that made it worse. A permanent anger. A girl had told me once that I looked like I ate puppies for breakfast and kittens for lunch.

Yeah, I know sweet words. But she wasn't far wrong. I hated the world and most things in it. I'd lost my parents. My older brother had taken off to sea, leaving me to basically raise myself. No problem, but it did create an anger that never seemed to go away. You add, anger to size, and throw in male youth. It just made people uneasy.

I held up my hands to the woman trying to show her I wasn't a threat. She relaxed enough to show me her dead phone and say, "I don't know."

Taking a deep breath, I tried to analyze what was happening. Where was the threat? What actions did I need to take? Attack or avoid. But none of it made any sense.

To top it off, I was jacked up on adrenaline before this even happened. I'd spent the morning sparring at the gym. Rolling with guys on the mat. Sparring always made me all hyper deep inside. I had to hold back to make sure I didn't hurt anyone, so my frustration just built.

It would take a couple of hours of quiet time at home before I could just be me again.

The woman was eyeing me then the door to the cab, obviously wondering if she could get back in and lock the door before I attacked.

Grumbling under my breath, I turned away as I tried to understand what was happening. I started analyzing things. I know some people would be surprised that a guy like me could think. At least that was the feeling I got. A big guy, an MMA fighter, dropped out of high school six months earlier, but I wasn't dumb, just not interested.

So I started going over what I knew. Saturday morning, spring, New York, planes falling, cars stopping, electricity out. There had been that flash of light, but I had just thought it was a reflection off a window or something. Cell phones out.

We weren't at war. At least not that I knew of. No alien ships hovering over the city.

Nope, it didn't make sense then a niggling thought at the back of my brain began to shove its way forward. No power, flash of light, everything stopping at the same time. EMP?

Nope, no way. It had to be something else.

A gut-worrying fear ate inside my insides. What now? I mean my older brother Johnny was off the coast of South Carolina. He wouldn't be home for a week.

I was still trying to figure it out when the Limo driver threw a punch at the cabbie. They'd been arguing ever since the crash. I watched and shook my head, he'd thrown a haymaker. He'd have done better with a couple of jabs. The cabbie leaned back and let the punch pass him by then threw two to the body and a third to the chin. The limo driver dropped to his knees.

One thing he should have learned years ago, don't get into a fight with a cabbie, they're tougher than boot leather.

Stepping back up onto the curb I started looking around. People where getting out of cars and cabs. Coming out of apartments and the bodega on the corner. Looking up at the sky, at each other. Confused, and concerned.

Some were obviously miles from home. Others separated from family. All of them looked scared.

Taking a deep breath, I turned and headed home. They were on there own. Just like everyone else. Individuals responsible for themselves. Not my problem man. I had more than enough problems to deal with. I didn't need to take on others.

Putting my head down, I started for home. People just naturally parted to let me through, giving me space.

I just wanted to get home, hole up, and forget about the world. They weren't my problem, I kept telling myself.

.oOo.

Haley

Have I told you how much I hate the dark? And a weak LED at the other end of a subway car does not qualify as light.

My stomach churned. The world had just ended, and I was trapped underground. Not a good feeling. A dozen dreads jumped through my mind. But I pushed them down and thought, I have to get out. Get out of being trapped. Get away from this constricting fear that was squeezing my chest.

And oh yeah, I needed to get out of town. Uncle Frank's call kept bubbling through my brain. Get away from the city. Was a huge wave rushing towards us? It was too easy to imagine it swooping down and filling the subways.

The thought of drowning made me want to scream. Drowning in the subway seemed so stupid. Jumping up, I started pulling at the doors. I needed to get out.

"Honey," An older Black woman said. "Give them time. They'll get it fixed."

A burning urge to yell at her filled me. I wanted to scream, You don't understand. But I ignored her and kept trying to pull the door open and failed miserably.

No one got up to help. Most of them were on their phone. Useless down here.

"Ug," I groaned as I gave up and started towards the front of the car, adjusting my backpack. People pulled their feet back. Afraid of interacting with the crazy girl. Several tried to give me a reassuring smile. But they didn't understand. I needed to get out.

The front door between cars opened. I stepped out onto the in-between-car platform then pushed the curtain screen aside and looked up and down the dark tunnel. My stomach clenched with pure fear. More darkness.

There was just enough light seeping out of the subway cars to see a second set of tracks disappearing around a curve.

Grabbing the handrail I stepped down onto the cinder then shivered when I thought about the third rail. Then laughed at myself. There was no electricity. I didn't have to worry about taking the wrong step and electrocuting myself.

Taking a deep breath, I decided to head north. It was the direction I needed to go. But everything was just so dark and smelled of oil and mold. The soft drip of water falling from the overhead the only sound. Swallowing hard, I tried to ignore the smell and took my first step, and almost tripped over a railroad tie.

"Damn," I cursed as I grabbed the side of the car to stop from falling. How was I going to make it to the next station if I couldn't even take a step without falling? Once again, my insides curled in on themselves as a pure terror ate at me. I needed to get out. But that meant facing my greatest fear.

Phone, you idiot, I thought as I pulled out my phone and used the flashlight feature to see my way. Obviously, whatever knocked out the

22

subway system hadn't reached down here to our phones.

People were in their seats. I could see them as I passed and wondered if I should tell them what had happened. That they would sit there until the end of time if they waited for the transit authority to fix things.

When I passed the front of the train the motorman stuck his head out of the window and yelled, "Hey, you can't do that."

I ignored him, focusing on getting out as I pushed the fear down. Ignore the fear, I kept telling myself. It's not real. You aren't being crushed. Just one step in front of the other. Keep moving. Over and over I said to myself, just keep moving.

A confidence was beginning to build inside of me with each step. I was getting closer. I was acting. I honestly thought I was going to make it. But then, a rat decided he needed to run across my feet.

Not just any rat, but one of those big ones. The King of rats.

The echoes of my scream are probably still rumbling through the subway system. I jumped, kicked, and screamed all at once.

Mr. King Rat jumped away then turned, baring his teeth, telling me that I'd stepped into his world, and he was perfectly willing to kill me at any time.

I, being the brave person I am, ran. Ran as fast as I could. Too terrified to think straight. Just determined to get away. To get out.

Only when my side began to hurt did I slow down, amazed I hadn't tripped and fallen a dozen times. Maybe terror gives people better balance. But I'd gone around a long curve. The train and therefore Mr. King Rat were long behind me and far out of sight.

"Slow down," I gasped as I forced myself to slow to a quick walk. A squeaking off to my left sent a shiver down my spine as I imagined the rats gathering in a conference to figure out a way to take down the crazy girl.

Biting down on my teeth, I forced myself to ignore the fear. Get out, I said, over and over. One step. Another.

I don't know how long I walked, ten minutes, ten hours. There is no telling, my mind didn't work that way anymore. All that mattered was taking the next step. But finally, I heard a new noise up ahead.

Freezing, I twisted to listen, terrified I was walking into a new danger. But I didn't have a choice. It was either forward, or back past Mr. King Rat and that wasn't happening. So I took a deep breath and started again. A minute later I realized the sound was people talking.

And then a weak light sent a burst of hope through me. The next station. It had to be people on the platform waiting for the train that would never come. Enough light spilled down from the station opening onto the platform.

A guy in his forties in a three-piece suit was staring at his phone when his eyebrows shot up seeing me down on the tracks.

I giggled with relief. People, not rats. A way out.

His frown deepened then he bent down and held out his hand to help me up onto the platform. I could see it in his eyes. I was a stupid girl who didn't know enough not to go down on the train tracks.

"Thanks," I said as I grabbed his hand and let him pull me up.

He continued to frown at me, obviously wanting an explanation about how I could be so dumb.

I was tempted to just ignore him but instead, I said, "The world has ended. Power's not coming back."

He laughed and I could see the relief in his eyes. I had been categorized. Crazy, weird girl, no threat, of course, she was down on the tracks. Crazy.

I let out a long breath and pushed past him. Get out. Get out of the subway, get out of the city.

My flashlight phone showed me the steps leading up to a glorious light. Sunlight. That most wonderful of all lights.

I jogged up the steps two at a time, determined to be free of my nightmare.

When I stepped out, I let out a long sigh. I was free. Free at last. Only to realize I'd stepped into a new nightmare.

Chapter Three

Tanner

I saw her step out of the subway station and froze for a second. Too many things were off. First, she was beautiful. Not unusual for New York, but still gut-punching. Heart-shaped face touched by the angels. Long blond hair in a ponytail, blue eyes. The girl next door look. Yes, unusual for New York. Next was the gray peacoat. Warm for the spring. And the book backpack looked like it'd been stuffed with enough to last a month of Sundays.

She was about fifty feet in front of me and just stood out from all the crowd. You know what I mean. Everyone else was still dazed, looking for others to solve their problems. But not this one.

Frowning, she twisted and took it all in. People arguing, staring at blank screens. A baby crying in the distance. It took her a good three seconds to accept it all then I saw a determination cross behind her eyes as she turned and headed north.

We were headed in the same direction. I, being a guy, just naturally followed the sweep of her peacoat back and forth as I shook my head at myself. The world was ending, and I was thinking about a girl's butt.

I mean, how stupid can a guy be? I looked down and focused on figuring out what I was going to do when I got home. How long would we be without power? The nights were cool, but I could get by without heat and the air conditioner hadn't worked for two years.

What about the refrigerator? I was trying to remember what food was in the house when something made me look up in time to see two guys dragging peacoat girl into an alley.

A dozen thoughts flashed through my mind. I mean it was brazen. Mid-day? Even in this neighborhood was risking something. Then I realized maybe not. No cops? No 911 for neighbors to call. Everyone confused, worried about their own survival.

My gut fell. Do not get involved, I told myself then scoffed. I couldn't ignore this. Who, what, why danced through my mind as I hurried. And I'll admit that hyper animal buried deep inside of me woke up, a fight. I'd been looking for one for weeks. Smiling, I turned into the alley.

The tall skinny guy had a hand over her mouth and a knife to her throat pulling her back down the alley. He leaned in and whispered something to her.

She cringed, her face turned white as a look of pure terror took her.

The second guy was maybe as heavy as me, but fat, not muscle. Both in their twenties. They looked like they came from this neighborhood which meant they knew how to fight. The fat guy was glaring at her, waiting his turn.

Okay, a knife changed things a bit, And two guys would make it tough. But then I saw the fear in her eyes and my heart sort of turned over. Then those beautiful eyes saw me and grew even bigger, filling me with more fear. My insides fell. One look at me and she assumed I was one of them. A big monster. The kind that couldn't be beaten.

I swear I was almost tempted to turn around and leave her to her fate. But like I said, I'd been looking for a fight.

"Hey," I yelled. I know, not very original.

Skinny guy stopped, his eyes narrowing as he glared at me, "Get your own."

I smiled and dropped my gym bag as that permanent anger at the bottom of my gut rose up demanding to be let loose. The world was going to hell and these two were making it worse.

No, I told myself. Get her away, that was the important thing. Not hurting them. Although, a possible side benefit.

"Let her go," I said. Again, I was going to have to work on my banter. I should have said something cool, pithy.

He pressed the knife against her neck, daring me to make my move.

I shrugged. "If you kill her, there won't be anyone to hide behind."

Heavyset guy frowned as he pulled a butterfly knife, flicked it open, and stepped towards me.

Okay, I thought as my left hand moved to protect my stomach. They weren't going to make this easy.

Peacoat girl stared at the heavyset guy's knife then back at me. I think she was realizing I was not here to hurt her. She silently pleaded with me, begging me to help her.

I pushed her out of my mind as I focused on the big guy in front of me. He circled, looking for an opening. I stepped back wanting to pull him away from his friend then faked going for the hand holding the knife.

He grinned and swiped at me. I backed off and let his arm pass me then grabbed at it. Only I think he knew what I was going to do before I did it and swung back catching me in the left forearm.

A sharp sting ran down my arm sending a bolt of worry through me. The guy was better than he looked.

My coach Gordy used to tell me that everyone has a plan until they get punched in the face. I'd just been hurt. That angry beast inside of me erupted as the world turned red. Ignoring the risk I yelled and charged. Kill. All I

31

wanted to do was put my hands around this man's throat and squeeze the life out of him.

His eyes grew three sizes as he brought the knife down in front to catch my charge. I ignored him, coming in close then shifted to his right and got his knife wrist before he could get back.

Now I had him, I thought as I smiled and looked him square in the eyes as I squeezed. Like I said, I'm two forty of solid muscle.

He tried to pull away then swung a left that caught me on the chin.

I shook it off and squeezed harder. The pain in his eyes became full of fear as he looked down at his wrist then back up at me.

Slowly, I bent his arm until his knife was facing back at him. He shoved back with every bit of his strength, but it wasn't enough as I slowly started to push it forward until the tip reached his shirt.

He freaked and tried to twist away but I didn't let him. I twisted him and pushed him up against the brick building while still trying to shove that knife into his chest.

His eyes grew bigger and bigger then then he finally got smart and dropped the knife. It was either that or die on the spot.

The tinkling of metal hitting pavement was what I had been waiting for. I instantly reversed course on the wrist and heard a loud snap.

The guy sucked in a huge breath to scream just as I bought my head forward in a classic headbutt, catching him square on the nose.

He dropped like a wet dish towel.

Standing over him I sucked in deep breaths waiting for him to get up. My heart pounded in my chest. My hands cramped into fists as the beast deep inside of me demanded I finish him off.

"NO!" The girl mumble screamed through the hand over her mouth.

I turned to see skinny guy trying to drag her down the alley away from me. She was twisting and struggling, but the knife at her throat restricted her movement.

"Like I said, let her go. It's your best chance."

He didn't drop her and scurry away like I hoped. Nope. Guys from around here did not run from fights. Instead, he tried to maneuver around some trashcans, glancing over his shoulder then back at me as I marched towards him.

"I'll kill her," he said, and I saw the truth in his eyes.

"Maybe," I said, "But then you die."

For a brief moment, I think he saw the truth in my eyes. If he hurt her, he died. I think he might have let her go, but she chose that moment to bite the hand covering her mouth.

He yelled then back handed her, knocking her to the ground.

A calm filled me. Gordy called it my monster calm. That rational part of me that took over in a fight when I got beyond the beast and saw what was going to happen. This man was going to die for hurting her.

He looked down at her, shaking his hand, then realized what he had done, jettisoning his only protection. Turning, he was going to run but I was on him too fast.

Swinging back with his knife he tried to slice me open like a fish. I scooted back, sucking in my stomach, then reached down and had one hand around his knife wrist, the other around his throat, and proceeded to lift him up off the ground.

His eyes bugged out as he fought for air.

I just smiled at him, slowly squeezing, waiting for nature to take its course.

Slowly he turned red, then purple, then finally, his head slumped as he passed out. The knife dropped.

Still, I held him, debating if I should let him live or not. It would be so easy to just keep squeezing until my fingers met in the middle. I wasn't thinking about cops, the law, or the trouble I might get in. I was past that.

But the girl scrambled to her feet, looking at me like I was Godzilla here to destroy her town.

Something in that look told me she would think less of me if I killed this man, so I dropped him, letting him crumple at my feet.

The girl stared at him, then at the other man still out, then at the two knives littering the alley then back at me. There was something in her eyes I couldn't read. Then her brow furrowed as she looked at my arm.

"You're bleeding."

"Really? I didn't know." I snapped with a sarcastic tone.

She frowned then stepped forward and grabbed my arm to turn it over. I'll admit, I was surprised. She'd been assaulted, dragged into a back alley and she was worried about me. "Are you okay?"

Glaring up at me she shook her head. "Sure, this happens to me all the time. I'm used to it."

For a moment I thought she was serious then realized she had her own sarcasm.

Twisting my arm, she examined it then shook her head. Dropping her backpack she quickly pulled out a T-shirt and wrapped it around my arm, holding it in place she said, "You need to see a doctor."

I laughed. "Not happening today. I think they've got bigger problems."

She didn't fight me on it. Instead, her eyes said she understood the world was ending.

I was still trying to figure out what to do next when heavy-set guy started to moan and twist on the ground. "Come on," I said as I handed her the backpack, grabbed my gym bag, and pushed at her lower back to get her moving. "These guys have got friends, and I don't want to be here when they show up."

Still holding the T-shirt wrapped around my arm she nodded and asked, "Do you live around here? I'll help get you home."

I swear, I think she was worried about me fainting from the loss of blood. It was sweet. I took a deep breath. Home, if you could call it that.

Chapter Four

Haley

My insides continued to shake. I will never forget the feel of that cold knife next to my throat. The knowledge that I was about to die. An hour into the end of the world and I had failed. Uncle Frank would be so disappointed in me.

I'd been taken off the street. Oblivious to the danger, focused on getting out.

A cold shiver ran down my spine when I thought about what those two had planned for me. The creep had actually whispered in my ear what he was going to do. I'd been so helpless. So weak.

Then this Hulk showed up out of nowhere. At first, I had thought he was one of them and I knew there would be no getting away. I can still remember the thought of wondering if I should just give in and hope to live. A thought that I am not proud of, but it was there.

Of course, I'd been wrong. So wrong. He wasn't my attacker but my hero. I still couldn't believe he'd taken those two apart like they were bugs to be dispatched. A mere hinderance. I don't think I ever felt so happy to see the skinny one lifted up off the ground. The look of pure fear in his eyes as he realized he wasn't going to win. Wasn't going to get me. And was at the complete mercy of the man who held him by the neck.

God, I held onto that memory. That sense of justice. It was going to help me get past this.

Mr. Hero had been cut. He'd gotten a six-inch gash on the inside of his arm. The kind that needed a dozen stitches. But he was right. Hospitals and doctors were going to be too busy to see him. And I needed to get out of town.

Get him home to his people, I thought. He deserved that much from me.

"To the right," he said as we approached the end of the alley.

I nodded as I held his arm, keeping pressure on the wound.

As we stepped out onto the street, I quickly saw that things hadn't changed. I'd almost been raped and killed, and the rest of the world was going on as if it had more important things to worry about. And really, it sort of did.

People were lost, confused. Those far from home were realizing things weren't going to come back quickly and were starting for home. Others were out on the street trying to figure out what had happened.

Oh, if they only knew. My heart ached as I realized how unprepared they were. None of them were working to get out of the city. How long did we have? Had the asteroid hit the Pacific like Uncle Frank predicted? If it had hit in the Atlantic, we would never get far enough away so there wasn't much use worrying.

"Listen," Mr. Hero said. "I can get home. You don't have to come."

I frowned up at him. I mean way up. The man was the size of a small building. Why didn't he want me to help? Did he somehow know about my need to get out of the city? No, it was something else. I could see a nervousness in his eyes that surprised me.

"Just be quite," I said dismissively. "You're losing blood and probably not thinking straight."

He frowned at me, and I thought he was going to snap back at me, but he bit his tongue then pointed to an old apartment building. Not the nicer part of town but then I'd known that as soon as I got up out of the subway.

Still holding his arm, I opened the door and helped him up three flights of stairs. And yes, I was perfectly aware I was alone with a strange man in a weird new world. Was I jumping out of the frying pan into the fire? Those two creeps in the alley had changed me. Put a permanent fear into my stomach.

But a guilty debt filled me. This man was hurt because of me. He'd risked his life. He deserved my help. And yes, I knew I was losing time. I needed to go, a conflict fought inside of me. Help? Run?

I decided to help, maybe it was wrong, but it is what I decided.

40

"Okay, I'm here," he said as we stopped in front of an old wooden door with the number 37 in brass centered.

I looked up at him and raised an eyebrow, I wasn't letting him go until I knew he was in good hands.

He sighed heavily then pulled out his keys and opened the door.

I was greeted by a dark apartment with just a faint light coming in from around the blinds on the window.

"You're parents aren't here?"

He scoffed and shook his head. "They died five years ago. My brother's a merchant sailor, at sea."

My heart broke. I knew what it was like to lose both your parents. I'll be honest, I'm not proud of my next thought which was, no one here meant I would have to stay long enough to fix him up. I was losing time.

I swear he could read my mind because he said, "I'm home. You can go."

Frowning, I said, "Shut up," then pushed him into a chair next to a dining table and placed his good hand onto my pretend bandage, and said, "Hold this,"

He just stared at me but finally, he did what I told him and held the T-shirt wrapped around his arm.

I opened the blinds to let in more light. Then saw all the blood on my hands and cringed before wiping them on my jeans. I'd change later. Turning I saw an apartment that looked like it had seen better days. Old furniture, a load of laundry folded on the end of a threadbare couch.

"You live here all alone?" I asked.

He shrugged, "Mostly, except when Johnny is in town."

"For five years?"

Again he shrugged. "Family services doesn't get involved unless someone reports things. And people around here don't talk to the authorities. Thank God for rent control."

I swear, it was like getting hit upside the head as I tried to understand. A boy of what thirteen? fourteen? being left alone to raise himself. An intermittent brother to watch over him. An appreciation for Uncle Frank filled me. When disaster had hit me, my Uncle was there to pick up the pieces. Even in his own grief, he made sure the four of us were taken care of. A shoulder to cry on, a hand to help. Always a rock in a raging river.

Okay Haley, I said to myself, get this guy fixed then get on the road.

"Do you have first aid stuff?"

He nodded, "The bathroom, down on the left."

I dumped my coat and backpack on the couch then used my phone light to find what I needed. I bundled it all up with a couple of towels then piled it all on the table next to him. I could feel him watching me as I went into the kitchen and got some water in a bowl.

The big silent type, I thought. Just rescue damsels in distress then not say anything for an hour.

"Here," I said as I gently began to peel the T-shirt away from his arm and cringed at the nasty wound.

He calmly looked at it then up at me, expecting me to fix it all. I wanted to scream. What did I know about wounds like this? I mean, I'd grown up with Chase and Ryan, they were getting hurt all the time. I swear, Chase had been taken to the emergency room a dozen times before he was twelve. But others had always fixed them.

Yet, I had learned enough. Purify, keep it clean, keep it bound up. "This is going to hurt," I said as I prepared to pour peroxide over the wound.

He cringed as the liquid hit the wound.

I had to bite down hard to stay focused. I hate hurting people. And even giants like him had to feel pain. Once I was sure the wound had been cleaned out, I lathered it with Neosporin then used a dozen band-aids to keep it closed before I wrapped it in gauze and finally an ace bandage.

"You need stitches or it's going to scar," I said as I looked up from the wound to find him staring at me. I swear, our eyes locked. But I'd just come out of a harrowing experience and wasn't in the mindset to become lost in a cute guy's eyes.

Shaking my head, I stepped back and looked at him, really looked. Like I said, a small giant. Maybe six-five. Black hair, and strange gray eyes that didn't seem to miss anything. And arms the size of railroad ties with a thick chest and shoulders the width of a truck.

Not really my type, I thought. I was more into the artsy type. This guy had jock written all over him. A Viking jock at that. But there was something in his look that made my insides sort of flutter. Not a bad flutter.

Maybe it was just the fact that he'd saved me. And then it hit me. Just how close I had come. Suddenly, my hands began to shake as I fought to keep myself under control and failed miserably. I couldn't stop the tears.

Everything hit me all at once. Uncle Frank's call and the thought I might never see him again. Worrying about Chase, Ryan, and Cassie. Mr. Rat in the subway. That cold knife at my throat. Oh yeah, and the end of the world. It all hit me. I put my face in my hands and began to cry as I turned away from him.

My shoulders shook as I couldn't stop the tears.

Mr. Hero didn't get up and put his arm around me. Didn't tell me that everything would be all right. He just sat there like a lump on a log and waited for the silly girl to pull herself together. I swear, an anger filled me. Anger at the world. Anger at the monsters who had attacked me. And yes, anger at this guy who had just seen me lose it.

Finally, I pulled myself together then sniffed as I wiped my nose with my sleeve. "I'm sorry."

He shrugged, "You've got a good reason."

That was it. Somehow it seemed so inadequate. Taking a deep breath I said, "You do know that the world's ending. About the asteroid hitting us?"

He sighed, "I wondered what it was."

"The power's not coming back. My Uncle said there might be an EMP. Do you know what that is?"

His brow furrowed. "Just because I'm big doesn't make me an idiot."

My stomach clenched, I swear my mouth has a mind of its own sometimes. "I'm sorry. I just …"

"Never mind," he said as he waved his good arm. "Where were you headed." He examined me for a second then said, "Let me guess, central park west?"

45

The rich part of town. Is that what he saw? Not a girl from Oklahoma? Not a scared senior in High School? "No, I need to get out of the city. You should too."

He laughed, not a snicker, but a burst of laughter then he frowned and said, "Are you crazy? Is it just today or have you been this delusional for a long time?"

My back stiffened as I stared back at him. "For a non idiot, you aren't thinking. There could be tidal waves. Tsunamis."

He shook his head. "Maybe, but you won't get far enough away before they hit."

"It's only about eight more miles to the George Washington Bridge."

Scoffing, his brow narrowed. "What makes you think you can make it that far? You couldn't get a hundred yards past the subway. And where are you going to go if by some miracle you get to the other side?"

"Idaho," I answered as I felt my face blush. Even I knew that now I sounded like the idiot.

His frown deepened as if he was having difficulty understanding what I said.

"Think about it," I said as I began to fight to justify myself. "The city is going to run out of food in about a week. Followed by a couple million tons of garbage and dead bodies. No working toilets. Disease is going to race against famine to see which can kill the most. Those creeps today will become the norm. This city, all the cities, will become a death zone."

He continued to stare at me for a long moment then sighed heavily. "Do you have a machine gun I don't know about? No? Then, you'll never make it. A pretty girl like you. Sorry, but you don't have a chance."

Anger flashed through me. How dare he tell me I wouldn't make it. All because I was a girl. But at the same time, I sort of knew he was right. I had seen it today. A knife against a neck will make a girl open her eyes and see the new reality.

"Come with me," I said. Again, my mouth with a mind of its own. "We might make it. Together."

Okay, my insides wanted to back pedal that statement. I swear I sounded sort of desperate. Okay, a lot desperate.

His head tilted as he stared at me, searching for the truth behind my requests. "So you need a bodyguard."

I shrugged, "You look the part. Think about it, It will be easier to survive the end of the world in Idaho."

Slowly his eyes traveled over me, and he smirked, "What's in it for me?"

Suddenly I thought of those creeps in the alley and shuddered. "If you think I'm going to sleep with you just to get you to go. Now you're the crazy one."

"So, let me see if I have this correct. I am supposed to risk my life, so you don't get hurt. Put my body on the line. But your body is too special. I get it. I'm just a dumb jock. I'm not an important person like you."

"NO!" I snapped. He didn't understand. "It's just ..."

He held up a hand. "Don't worry about it, Besides, you're not my type anyway."

A dozen thoughts wormed their way through my brain as I tried to understand what he meant by that. But I immediately realized my priority. Getting to Idaho, and this giant might be the only person in this world that could help me make that happen.

He continued to frown at me then said, "We'll never make the bridge tonight. We'll leave first light."

Chapter Five

Tanner

I grabbed Johny's Jack Daniels out of the back of the cupboard and poured myself three fingers. As I threw it back, I saw the girl staring at me like I was committing murder.

"Hey, my arm hurts," I said as I poured another drink then lifted the bottle. "Do you want some?"

I swear, you'd think I'd asked her to kill a kitten. "No thank you."

Shaking my head, I bit back a laugh. The world was ending, and she was worried about being judged by people. I knew the type, so worried about what other people thought. Especially family. And I could tell, she had a strong family. I could always spot them. Assured. There is something about knowing you're loved that makes a person confident in themselves.

"My name is Haley," she said, "Haley Conrad."

"Like the comet?" I asked.

She looked down for a moment then said, "Actually, yes. I was named after the comet. But with one L, not two."

I nodded as an awkward silence crept into the air. Why had I agreed to go with her? I mean, walking to Idaho. No way were we going to make it. But she had been right. This city without electricity would become a death trap.

Looking over the top of my glass I studied her for a moment. Cute and pretty, two different things. Assured. Built perfectly. But how could she think we'd survive?

As if reading my mind she shrugged, "What choice do we have? If there is a better plan, I'm willing to listen. But think long term. A farm in the middle of nowhere is our best chance."

Nodding, I took a deep breath then finished my drink, rinsed out my glass and left it in the sink then said. "If you're hungry, you can grab whatever you want, I'll be back in a few minutes."

Her eyes grew three sizes, "You're leaving?"

I nodded, it was weird, I wasn't used to having to explain where I was going or why. So, me being me, I just ignored her and headed out the door.

"What's your name?" she called from behind me.

"Tanner Parks," I told her as I closed the door behind me. But I'd seen the frustration and the beginning of anger in her eyes. She was a pretty girl. That meant she wasn't used to being ignored. Oh well, she was going to have to learn.

When I got to Mrs. Freemont's door, I knocked. A dozen locks unlocking later the door cracked open. The sweetest old lady in this part of New York smiled then opened it wide. Stepping back for Jordan to rush out, his tail windmilling a mile per minute, fighting every urge to jump up on me.

"Hey boy," I said as I rubbed his head.

He curled into me, celebrating the pack becoming one again. My heart ached. This dog was the only thing that had ever loved me. A Golden Retriever I'd found as a puppy digging through a dumpster after a rat. Tangled fur, a nasty cut on his haunch. One look and we'd fallen in love.

Four years later and we were still best friends.

"Thank you, Mrs. Freemont," I said as I continued to pat Jordan. "Um. Did you hear about the asteroid?"

The old woman frowned at me.

"That's why the power is out. It's not coming back on."

"It hit the power station?" She said in surprise. "They'll fix it. I remember the blackouts in '65 and '77. It only takes them a day to fix it. I'll just stay off the streets."

My heart fell as I realized there was nothing I could do. The woman couldn't walk to Idaho. She wouldn't go no matter what I told her.

"I don't think they're going to fix this one. You might think about going to your son's. But you'll have to walk. The subways are out."

"Jacob? They live in Queens. Why would I go there."

"Think about it," I said as I tapped my leg for Jordan to follow me. "I'm leaving in the morning. I won't be coming back. Thank you for watching Jordan for me. He's going to miss you."

Her eyes grew very big as she studied me then Jordan. I think it was beginning to sink in. The seriousness of what was going on.

"Maybe I will go see Jacob. His wife, she doesn't do well when things don't work. The only cooking she knows is calling those Uber people."

I smiled sadly, we would be leaving early. This would be the last time I saw this woman. It sort of hit me, I was leaving everything I knew. Johnny would come back and find me gone. What would he think? Me, farming in Idaho.

He'd laugh his butt off then send up a silent prayer of thanks that he didn't have a kid brother to worry about anymore. Then finish off the bottle of Jack Daniels before getting a hold of one of his girlfriends and sitting back to enjoy what remained of the world.

A sadness hit me. Who was I kidding? He'd never get back. If his ship somehow made shore, no way was he walking all the way up here.

There wasn't enough around here to justify the effort.

"It's just you and me," I said as I ruffled Jordan's fur. "Well, and this cute girl. But don't worry. If she gives us a hard time, we'll just dump her and head off on our own."

Jordan wagged his tail, obviously agreeing with everything I said.

When I opened the door, he rushed in and froze when he saw Haley in the dim light then like every Golden Retriever ever born rushed to meet his new best friend.

She blanched for a second then dropped to her knees to give my dog a hug. I swear, she'd made a lifelong friend in about two seconds.

Jordan looked at me, his tongue hanging from his mouth. A new pack member. It is about time.

"Jordan, this is Haley. She's taking us to Idaho. Just think about all the trees put there just for you."

She looked up and smiled slightly.

My guts tightened as I realized just how pretty she was. Careful Tanner, I said to myself, or she'll have you wrapped around her little finger.

"One condition," I told her "For me going. I'm in charge."

She frowned, then laughed at me. "Um. NOOO."

I shrugged, "Do you have a lot of experience fighting? How many times have you been punched in the face? I'll be honest. You were taken in about two minutes after coming up out of the subway."

She frowned. "You saw me leave the subway."

Crap, I'd been caught. I shrugged. "You were hard to miss. Clueless, walking into danger. One of the reasons I should be in charge."

Her frown deepened as she thought about it. "We can talk about it later. But when it comes to fighting. Yes, you are in charge. But everything else, we'll talk about it."

I laughed and started getting myself a huge bowl of cereal. I'd poured the last of the milk then realized I hadn't offered her any. She just shook her head then said, "We need to figure out what we're taking with us. Food, I guess. Weapons. Do you have a gun?"

"In this town? No. I could get one, or I could have it before this morning. Now, I'm not so sure."

She sighed, then spent the next ten minutes telling me everything I should take. Everything from flashlights to pots and pans.

When she finally ran down, I just said, "You'd have me packing about half the apartment. I can't fight carrying a refrigerator on my back. I need to keep my hands free."

Pausing, she looked off into the distance then asked, "Do you really think it will be difficult."

Okay, no way she could be that naive, "A beautiful girl, two people with packs probably filled with food. No cops, no law, nothing stopping anyone…"

"One look at you and they won't dare bother us."

Now it was my time to laugh, "I can take two, maybe three. But more than that and I'll get overwhelmed. This isn't like the movies. Guys around here know what they're doing. And there is always the shot to the back of the head and I'm off the board and you're on your own."

Her face grew white as she realized what I was saying was true.

As if my words had changed something in her, she shut up, her eyes wandering off, thinking, worrying.

I finished my cereal and said, "My arm is killing me. I'm going to finish that bottle of Jack and crash. I'll wake you in the morning. Early."

Her brow furrowed as she glanced at the bottle on the counter then at the sun still peeking around the blind.

"You can crash on the couch or my Mom and Dad's room at the end of the hall." Then I got up, rinsed out the bowl, and put it in the sink before grabbing the bottle with my good arm, tapping my leg for Jordan to follow me then headed back to my room.

I know. I wasn't being very sociable. So kill me.

But I took a swig then plopped down on my bed and stared up at the ceiling, hoping I'd fall asleep and wake up to discover this had just been a nightmare. But then I wouldn't have a pretty Haley Conrad in my apartment. Okay, not a complete nightmare.

Unfortunately, no such luck. I woke in the dark to remember every detail and shuddered.

Moonlight seeped in, enough to get up and move around. I grabbed my gym bag, dumped everything on the bed, and started loading it up with jeans, shirts, socks, and the picture on my dresser of my Mom and Dad.

When I hit the kitchen, I started stuffing food into the bag. Stuff that could last, cans of tuna, a couple cans of chili, a loaf of bread, the dry cereal. Then I threw in a pot and some knives and forks.

I was going to go back to Johnny's room and wake Haley when she came around the edge of the kitchen. My stomach dropped. She was standing there in long bare legs, wearing nothing but a T-shirt that barely covered the important parts.

And I swear. She had no idea what she was doing to me. If she knew, she wouldn't have let herself be seen like that. It was too risky. "Get dressed," I said, perhaps a little meaner than I needed to. "We've got to get going."

She frowned at me then asked, "Did you pack dog food."

"Yes," I lied then waited until she'd gone back to her room before scooping out a bunch of dog food into a trash bag and stuffing it into the corner of my bag.

I've got to give the girl credit, it didn't take long for her to get ready. Two minutes, tops, and she was pulling on her peacoat then shouldering her backpack. She frowned as she looked at me then said, "What are we waiting for."

Laughing, I opened the door for her then grabbed my bag, put the leash on Jordan, and followed her out. And yes, I knew I was crazy for doing this. A pretty girl asked me to help her get to Idaho and I said yes. I mean, I wasn't normally this stupid. But then this was a very pretty girl.

Just before I pulled the door closed behind me, I looked back at the note I'd left on the refrigerator and wondered if Johnny would ever find it.

Shaking my head, I pulled the door closed. For the first time in my life. I didn't lock it.

Chapter Six

<u>Haley</u>

The city was dead. Silent. Waiting like a cat at a mouse hole. Ready to pounce. A quick shiver shot down my spine as I thought about those two creeps in the alley the day before. Gritting my teeth, I looked up at the gray sky as I tried to push the fear away.

Then I looked over at Tanner and shook my head. What would have happened if he hadn't been there? Don't count on him, I reminded myself. I'd lain in bed last night and mapped out all the ways things could go wrong. This guy walking away was high on the list.

"We'll work our way down to the express way then head up. Fewer people," he said as he gently pulled at Jordan's leash to get him away from a light post.

All I could do was nod. Everything was happening so fast. The street was filled with empty cars. I shuddered, we needed to get out of here, out of this city. Everything was going to go so bad once people began to understand what had happened.

Again, I glanced over at Tanner and thought. He wasn't pretty. Handsome in that manly way. Square jaw, the small scar on his chin gave his face character. And I was relying on him to get me to my grandfather's farm.

And yes, I was very aware how stupid I had been, asking him to go. I mean, what happened when we were in some forest somewhere? All alone. Would he demand payment for his continued protection?

But he'd said I wasn't his type. What did that mean? I mean, most guys thought I was cute. At least cute enough.

I tried to forget his words and focus on getting out of the city. The air had a stillness to it. The sour garbage smell had gotten stronger over the night, and my stomach rumbled. We should have eaten before we'd left but he'd been in such a hurry.

When we got to the expressway we stood there for a minute and looked at all the cars. Two of them wrapped around each other.

"Where did the people go?" I asked.

He shrugged, not bothering to answer. That was so him. I was learning. The boy didn't know the meaning of small talk. God, it was going to be a long trip if he didn't talk. I mean, how could a person go through life not talking about what happened around them?

"I guess it didn't hit in the Atlantic, the asteroid," I said. "Or we'd be a hundred feet under water by now."

He simply nodded as he scanned the road ahead of us.

An anger flashed through me. "Really, you're not talking to me?"

He frowned and shook his head without looking at me, then sighed heavily. "I'm trying to see problems before they hit us."

Now it was my time to frown, "There's no one around."

He scoffed then pointed to the back of a car. A man in a business suit and no tie was waking up rubbing his eyes. Then Tanner pointed up the road to the other side of the expressway. Two boys about our age were working there way down the road, peeking into cars, obviously looking for anything valuable.

I'd been so focused on talking I hadn't even seen them. Cursing under my breath I promised myself to focus. This was how I ended up being dragged into an alley. I wasn't oblivious, just focused too far into the future instead of the here and now.

We wove our way through the cars and trucks as the sun came up over the city, its yellow light peeking through the buildings. The Hudson River off to our left. The ferries and boats were all gone. I wondered if they'd been washed out to sea.

Things were going good, I thought. We were making good time. Tanner hadn't been forced to scare anyone away. The first day in a long journey I thought to myself. But we'd be over the bridge and into New Jersey before dark.

Suddenly, Jordan twisted around and started barking. Both Tanner and I looked behind us and froze. A wave of water thirty or forty feet high was rushing up the river.

"Run," Tanner yelled as he grabbed my arm and forced me forward.

My heart raced as my mind tried to figure it out. Twenty-four hours for the wave to travel through the pacific, around Cape Horn, or through the Indian Ocean and up the coast of first South America then up North America.

How was this possible? What kind of force must it have taken?

"Hurry," Tanner yelled as he looked over his shoulder.

I glanced back and felt my stomach drop with pure fear. It was too close. We'd never outrun it.

As if reading my mind, Tanner raced to the edge of the parkway, looked over then picked up Jordan and jumped.

"No," I yelled only to find him on top of a parked car holding up his hands for me. I didn't hesitate, that wave was going to kill me. I jumped and let him catch me. He didn't do anything cute or sexy. You know, hold me. Instead, he swung me off the car, jumped, and began running.

I raced after him terrified, my backpack punching me with every step.

A constant roar behind me made me glance over. The water was rushing up the street, picking up cars and tossing them aside like kid's toys. If the water didn't drown us, the cars would crush us.

"Here," Tanner yelled as he pulled a trashcan on the corner. He lifted it only to be stopped by a chain. This was New York after all. If it wasn't chained down it would be stolen.

Tanner growled under his breath, then grunted as he tugged at it, snapping the chain. In one swift move, he threw the trashcan through an office building's plate glass window. "Go," he yelled as he pushed me into the building.

I stepped over broken glass as a car was lifted up behind us.

Without warning, Tanner picked me up, threw me over his shoulder, and ran, hitting the stairs two at a time. Jordan at his heel.

Lifting up, I saw the water rushing past the building, spilling in through our opening, rushing towards us. Tanner climbed another flight of stairs then turned to look down into the lobby.

"Hey," I said as I patted at his back, I needed to see.

He slowly lowered me down without taking his eyes off the water.

I turned and watched as the water continued to pour in, washing halfway up the first flight of stairs. Tearing up the receptionist's desk and pushing it into a far wall. The planters with ferns were smothered as the water rushed into every crevasse.

Both of us stood there, unable to believe the force, the destruction.

Tanner shook his head. "No warning. People didn't know this was coming."

I suddenly thought about that man in the car, those two boys looking to steal stuff. People in their homes. Both here, but also along the beaches up and down the coast. How many people died today?

Suddenly I began to grow mad as I remembered being tossed over his shoulder like a bag of potatoes. "Hey, next time, don't man handle me. I can run just as fast as you."

He rolled his eyes then said, "I'll think about it."

Grinding my teeth I ignored him. This was who he was, I realized. Other people's opinions didn't matter. It was like he was an island on his own, not needing people. Not worried about other people's opinions.

God, it was going to be a long trip.

"We'll crash here," he said as he pointed to an office. "Let the water recede. It might take a day or two."

"We have to get out of the city," I snapped. "Two days and we've made a mile and a half."

He let out a long breath then pointed to the water below. "If you want to swim to New Jersey, go ahead."

I hate being wrong almost as much as I hate the dark. And that smug look of his made me want to slap it off his face. But then it'd be like a gnat swatting at a building, pretty useless. So I turned and marched into the first office and dumped my backpack onto the couch.

Suddenly a crash down the hall made me jump. Rushing out to the staff's break area I saw Tanner pulling a chair out of a vending machine. He'd thrown it through the glass and was picking out bags of potato chips and candy bars.

"What are you doing?"

He shrugged those massive shoulders of his and said, "Getting breakfast."

I could only stare as he sat down at a table and began stuffing his face. What an animal. And to make it worse, he didn't get anything for me, instead making me pick through the broken glass to get a bag of Doritos.

We sat there in silence, both lost in our own world. The second day of almost dying. Would it be like this every day? What would try to kill us tomorrow?

"How long? Until the water drains away?"

He shrugged then opened a Milky Way.

"God, Tanner, can't you even be a little social?"

He paused then sighed heavily. "No. Probably not."

I fought to not role my eyes. Remember, I told myself, I needed this man. One, I thought I could trust him. I mean, I wasn't his type, remember? And there was no denying he looked scary enough to keep the ghouls and monsters at bay. No, I needed to make sure I didn't upset him.

I had to close my eyes and count to ten. Only when I was calm enough did I get up and go back to the office where I'd left my stuff. Thankfully, Jordan followed me.

"How is it possible," I said to the dog. "Such a troglodyte can have a cool dog like you?"

Jordan just wagged his tail then pushed his head under my hand demanding to be petted.

I sank to my knees to bury my face in his fur and let the tears flow. I'd almost died. Again. I was teamed up with a sulking idiot, and the world had only just begun to try and kill me. So of course I cried.

Sighing, I finally let Jordan go and curled up on the couch, waiting. I always seemed to be waiting. Every hour or so I'd go our and check the water. It was going down, draining back into the river. Until finally the lobby was semi-dry. Oh, everything was soaked, and the air smelled like the bottom of the Hudson. But we wouldn't drown.

Tanner found me staring at it then said. "We can go, maybe make a couple of miles before it gets dark. We'll find a place to hole up."

A surge of joy filled me. Action. We were moving forward, not waiting. I rushed back to get my stuff then joined him as we climbed down the stairs. Both of us stood at the broken windows and stared out at the new world outside.

Cars had been tossed around, piled up, store windows on both the first and second floors had been shattered. Doors ripped off businesses, and a layer of mud covering everything. A brown line eighteen feet high marked the flood's zenith.

We hadn't gone a dozen feet when a rat rushed out from behind a dumpster.

"How did they live," I asked.

Tanner laughed, "Rats and cockroaches. They always live. It is in their nature. And with all the bodies, there's going to be a rat population explosion. I wouldn't want to be around here in a couple of months."

I looked at him confused.

He shrugged, "Read a book, The Earth Abides, years ago. That was one of the things that happened. The rats started to take over the world until they didn't."

"You read a book?" I said mockingly. Like I've said, my mouth has a habit of flapping before my mind kicks in.

He glared at me then smiled. A smile that didn't reach his eyes. Okay, do not tease him about his intelligence, I thought as a shiver raced down my back. The man could break me in two without trying.

We continued on as an awkward silence engulfed us. Only Jordan's wagging tail stopped it from becoming too heavy. Things on 57th were no better. Mangled cars, broken windows. Two or three people came out to survey the damage. A homeless guy staring up at the sky. How had he survived?

Twice I saw bodies the water had left behind. One a forty-something mom wrapped around a light post. Another, a man in a suit laying dead on the steps to the subway.

Suddenly, Tanner stopped. I almost walked into him then peeked around him to see a massive yacht sitting in the middle of the intersection. One of those boats rich people have. Not some puddle jumper but a million-dollar job.

Tanner smiled at me and asked, "This EMP, do you think it hit outboard engines? I mean, they don't normally have computer chips."

My brow furrowed as I tried to understand his question. "Why. Idaho is sort of inland." I swear, I wasn't disparaging his geographical knowledge.

He growled at me as if I was too dumb to see the obvious then started for the big boat.

"The Zodiac," he said pointing to a small gray rubber boat tied to the top of the cabin. "They use it to get back and forth to shore. It will have an outboard engine."

"So?"

He let out a long breath as he tried to figure out a way up onto the boat. "So, if this works. We can go up the Hudson, across on the Erie canal, then down the Ohio, Mississippi, and up the Missouri. I mean, it's how the west was settled."

I stared at him, my jaw somewhere around my knees. How did he know this? And was it possible? We wouldn't spend the next two years walking across the continent. We could ride in style.

Somewhere deep in my heart, I doubted it would be that easy. And as it turned out, I was right.

Chapter Seven

Tanner

A small lightness filled me. Maybe, just maybe, I could make this work. I mean there were so many benefits. No walking. Being in the middle of the river we were away from people. Please, I begged as I jumped up and caught the railing to pull myself up onto the boat.

The yacht lay on its side at an angle, but I was able to work my way up and cut the boat loose, dropping it down to the street below. No engine though. And I wasn't rowing to Idaho.

It took me ten minutes to find the outboard engine stored down in the engine compartment along with a three-gallon can of gas.

"Here," I said to Haley as I leaned over and lowered the can to her.

"How are we going to get this to the river?" she asked with a frown.

I just smiled as I tossed the can of gas and my gym bag into the back of the small boat. Threw the engine over my shoulder and started dragging the boat towards the river.

Haley ran to catch up, her eyes huge as she watched me then looked at the boat.

Eight feet long, inflated rubber sides, a hard bottom. More than enough room.

"Will this work?"

I would have shrugged but the engine was getting heavy.

"If it doesn't, we've only lost an hour," I said as I concentrated on not slipping on the layer of mud covering the street.

When I finally got down to the river, we both gasped to see how things had changed. Every pier had been washed away. The water was filled with debris, wood, trash, and parts of boats. And finally, a body floated face first, bobbing as the river knocked it against a half-submerged foot ferry.

Haley cringed and stepped away. But she didn't freak. I've got to give her that. No crying. No demanding I save the dead person.

Ignoring the destruction, I focused on getting things set up. I pushed the boat into the water, attached the engine to the back of the boat, the can of gas, gave the squeeze bulb three pumps then pulled the starter cord.

Nothing.

I fiddled with the controls, making sure everything was set correctly, then pulled three times to prime the pump. I'd always been told that old-type engines would survive an EMP. It was the computer chips that got knocked out.

Lifting up, I glanced over to see a look of concern on Haley's face. Maybe just a hint of doubt. As if she thought there was no way a guy like me could make this work.

Gritting my teeth, I pulled again and felt the engine cough and sputter. "Almost," I said and pulled again.

The engine caught, sputtering then settling into a stead drone.

"What if it stops," Haley said, standing on the beach, hesitating.

I shrugged as I went through the gears making sure everything worked. "Then we float until we hit land."

She seemed to accept that.

"Or," I added, "We float out to sea, we die a slow death, and the last thing you ever see is my ugly face."

Her eyes widened. I couldn't help but smile, I'll admit, it was fun poking at her. The girl was too perfect. Holding out my hand, I helped her into he boat. Jordan jumped in, his tail wagging a mile a minute, looking forward to an adventure.

I reversed us out into the river then turned upstream. Hailey sat in the middle holding Jordan. Her wide eyes scanned the river then looked back at me.

Smiling wide, I let the air rush past me and tried to ignore the destruction along both sides of the river. More piers were gone, several buildings had been knocked down leaving rubble-filled patches of ground.

The river itself was crammed with junk. New Jersey and New York are not known for being clean. All of it had been washed back into the river. Twice I had to slow down to maneuver around half-submerged boats.

Another time I had to swerve to avoid a body. My gut tightened at the thought of hitting it and the prop getting mangled in human flesh.

Haley kept glancing back over her shoulder, obviously expecting me to screw up.

I ignored her, focusing on the river as my mind tumbled through a thousand thoughts. How far could I go on a can of gas? How long until dark? I didn't look forward to going upriver at night. I'd hit something and sink us faster than a New York minute.

When we passed under the GW bridge Haley looked back and raised an eyebrow before yelling back to me, "It would have taken us all day and most of the night to get this far."

I smiled then said, "If we weren't attacked and pulled into an alley."

She swallowed hard then focused forward, occasionally pointing out obstacles and dangers. The wind whipped her hair as she leaned down and hugged Jordan.

I kept the boat in the middle of the river. But I didn't have to worry. No one was coming out to get us. We were the least of the Coast Guard's problems. We were about five miles past Yonkers when the engine started coughing.

My gut fell as I tried to figure out what was going on. Haley looked back, her eyes the size of small moons.

Gulping, I picked up the gas can and gave it a good shake to hear a small slosh. "Crap," I mumbled as I pointed the boat to the east shore and tipped the can to get the last bit of gas.

Haley kept glancing back at me then at the approaching shore. "There," she yelled pointing to a wooded part of the shore. Twisted railroad tracks lay at the water's edge.

My mind tried to catalog everything. How far to people? That was my greatest fear. We were dropping into the unknown. Cops? Angry residents, river monsters, who knew?

The engine continued to sputter and cough, "Please," I begged, I didn't want to have to swim for it.

Barking like it had a bad cough, the engine gave one last gasp then quit. Holding my breath I waited as the boat continued to glide forward through an eddy. The beach was mangled with downed trees and twisted railroad tracks, ties thrown around like Lincoln Logs.

"There," Haley said as she pointed to a space between two downed trees lying in the water then. The wave had washed away six feet of the bank. I held my breath wondering if we were going to make it when she jumped out a yard from the beach, the water to her knees and pulled us up onto the shore. I shook my head, This girl was not a shirker.

Jordan jumped out, sniffed his thanks to Haley then found the first tree.

When I joined Haley on the beach I took a deep breath. "We screwed up?" I said as I looked at the forest around us.

She frowned up at me. I could see it in her eyes, I was the one who had come up with the plan. What was this we stuff?

"Blankets, a tent," I said to her. "I didn't think about spending the night outdoors. It's not something us New Yorkers do very often. I figured we'd find empty buildings."

The color began to drain from her face. I think she was realizing just how unprepared we were. "Maybe we could ask for help. There's got to be houses around here. Rich ones."

"Ha," I scoffed. No way the people around here were going to be putting out a welcome mat.

"Freeze," A gravelly voice yelled.

My gut clenched as I turned to see an old codger with a very big rifle pointed at my chest.

"This is private property. You got to leave."

I slowly brought my hands away from my waist. I didn't want this guy getting the wrong idea. Swallowing I tried to smile and failed miserably. His trigger finger tightened and I expected to be blown into the next county any minute.

"We're out of gas," Haley said, stepping next to me. Her voice had that innocent, butter-wouldn't-melt-in-her-mouth tone that only pretty girls can pull off. Look at me, I wouldn't hurt a fly.

The old man glanced at her then immediately back at me. Our eyes locked and I knew the guy was running through possibilities, kill me now and get rid of his problems was probably top of that list.

Of course, that was when Jordan decided that he'd found a new friend and approached him, tail wagging, tongue bouncing.

The man ignored my fierce guard dog and glared at me.

"If we can get gas we'll leave," I said.

He didn't bite, instead, he continued to stare, a cold, heartless stare that made my insides shake. This was not a nice man. The way he looked at Haley, the angry glare in his eyes. He wasn't mad at us for being there. He saw us as an opportunity.

Still glaring, he nodded over his shoulder.

I glanced at Haley, I was pretty sure the guy was telling us to go that way. Did he have gas? Or did he want us to get a shovel to dig our own graves? Who knew? The guy looked older than the Empire State Building. Tall, skinny, a two-day-old beard, jeans, flannel, wool cap.

Who was this guy? I mean, I'd always heard that the homes along the river were mansions. This guy looked like he'd fit in at Bob's pool hall down the street from home.

Shrugging, I tapped Haley on her lower back. We really didn't have a choice. But every nerve in my body was telling me this wasn't going to end well. We'd gotten out of the city only to end up with Elmer Fudd threatening to put a bullet through our hearts.

She glanced up at me, her eyes furrowed with worry.

I tried to give her my best reassuring smile while my mind worked on getting that gun away from this guy.

"Inside," the man said as we stepped out from the forest.

A large home, facing the river. It had to be twenty rooms. Three stories, Pretty much a mansion.

"Ain't no phone, no power," the old man said. "We're all alone." The words sent a chill down my spine. I swear, It was like a serial killer was taking us to his lair where he'd spend the next three days having fun with us.

Haley glanced over her shoulder, "An asteroid hit us, knocked out all the electricity. Everything."

"Hu," the man grunted.

Hailey glanced up at me and I knew she was thinking this guy was even less social than I was. But I saw the fear in her eyes. She was picking up the same vibe as me.

"I swear," I said, "If we can get gas, we'll get out of here."

"You first, girl," the man said as he jammed the gun barrel into my back.

Haley took a deep breath and reached for the doorknob. She opened the door onto her foot and cursed, bending at the waist to rub her injured toe.

If the old guy was any kind of man, his attention would be focused on the young female bent over in front of him. No man in the world could resist. It was what I had been waiting for.

I spun, catching the barrel of the rifle, keeping it away from Haley.

Unfortunately, I wasn't dealing with just any old guy. This guy knew what he was doing. Instead of fighting, he fired the rifle into the air, burning my hand then twisting and wrestling it out of my hands before bringing the rifle butt upside of my head.

Fortunately, He wasn't dealing with an idiot. I rolled with it, then twisted, threw an arm between his legs, and lifted him up and over to drop him in a Supplex.

At the last minute, I held up. I didn't need to break this guy's neck. Instead, I twisted the rifle out of his hands and stepped back.

He lay on the ground, scowling up at me, expecting me to shoot him where he lay. I've got to give it to him. He didn't beg or whimper. Just stared at me, waiting for me to put a bullet between his eyes.

"Tanner," Haley said as she put a hand on my arm. I swear, she thought I would actually shoot the old guy. What kind of monster did she think I was?

Chapter Eight

Haley

My heart raced while I waited for Tanner to come back to his senses. He'd erupted so quickly. Disarmed the man and was now fighting with himself about what action to take next.

"Please," I said as I gently pushed his arm down.

He let out a long breath then nodded and lowered the rifle.

I sighed, pleased he'd listened to me. The man wasn't a complete monster. There was something deep inside of him that allowed him to be kind, merciful.

Once I saw he had himself under control I turned back to the man on the ground and glared at him with my best angry face. "What's your name?"

"Is there anyone in the house," Tanner interjected, going to the important stuff first.

The man glared back, obviously wondering if he could get away somehow. I almost laughed at him. He was dealing with Tanner, one wrong move and he'd end up dead enough to join the people floating down the river.

Finally, he realized his only hope was in cooperating. "Nobody else."

Tanner told him to stand up then made him go into the house first. I followed. We'd come in through the kitchen that opened up to a living room with big picture windows looking out over the river.

Without thinking, I flicked the light switch. Of course, nothing. What now?

But Tanner had a plan. He made the guy sit in a kitchen chair then pulled the cord off a toaster and used it to tie the guy's hands behind his back. I could only shake my head. It would have taken me two weeks to work that coord off. He snapped it like it was a loose thread on a seam.

Once he had the man's hands secured, he let out a long breath and took the rifle back. "Watch him," he said. "Call me if he tries to get free."

I swallowed hard as he left me to search the house. I studied our prisoner and wondered about him. "This isn't your house. Is it?"

He glared back at me then shook his head. "No, my car broke down yesterday, just up the road. I came up here to ask for help. Found the place empty."

A cold sadness filled me. Some family had gone away for the week. Spring break. Maybe they were down in Florida. A beautiful home they might never see again.]

"Your boyfriend is a freak. You shouldn't be with him."

83

I didn't correct him on his mistake. Tanner would never be my boyfriend. I wasn't his type. Instead, I just studied the man, waiting. The more he talked the more he would reveal.

"Why don't you let me go? I swear, I won't hurt you."

Nothing, I gave him nothing, waiting.

"Please, "he begged. "He'll kill me."

That made me smile just a bit. "Maybe."

The guy's face drained of color as he began to realize I wasn't some easy pushover that could be manipulated.

Tanner stepped back into the kitchen and shot me a quick smile as he held up what looked like cords from a window blind. "The house is empty."

He then proceeded to tie the man up like a market hog in a butcher's shop window. Hands again, then feet, then everything tied to the chair itself. When he was done, he stepped back and glanced at me.

I swear, he was waiting for me to criticize him.

"Can you watch him a bit," he said. "I want to check out the grounds."

I nodded then pulled out a chair, laid the rifle on the table, and folded my arms. Our prisoner glared back at me. The two of us sat there. Jordan next to me, silently asking what new game this was and when was it his turn.

Tanner came back in with a wide smile. "There's a car in the garage. I can siphon some gas."

My heart relaxed. Tanner had been right, the river was our way out. We'd been safe until we hit the shore.

"Should we stay here tonight?"

Tanner glanced at our prisoner then nodded. "Yeah. We can also get blankets. First aid stuff, food. Anything you think we might need."

A cold awareness hit me. We were stealing. But the rules had changed. We needed stuff to survive.

"The stove is gas," I told him. "We can have a hot dinner."

He smiled, "And pancakes in the morning before we take off. You get started and I'll get our stuff from the boat. If I can find an extra gas can we'll double up, make sure we don't run out."

Tapping his leg for Jordan, he left me. I searched through the cupboards to see what I had to work with then opened the freezer. A roast was half thawed. Two days without power. I ended up making us broiled steaks with potatoes and asparagus.

Tanner pushed back from the dinner and smiled at me, obviously pleased. I knew he liked it because he had thirds.

"I'm glad I put off siphoning the gas. It would have ruined that meal."

A warmness filled my heart.

We spent the evening using flashlights we found in a junk drawer to search the house and get what we needed. Blankets, a pack to move Tanner's stuff from his gym bag, the flashlights, matches. A storm lantern was lit and set in the middle of the living room.

Tanner passed me with a huge smile, went out then came back with a sledgehammer and headed for a room at the end of the hall. A heavy clang made me jump. I rushed to the room to find him pounding the sledge at a tall metal cabinet.

"A gun safe," he said, shooting me a huge smile. My gut tightened. I knew guns would be helpful. Especially in this new world but that didn't mean I liked it.

Another swing with the big hammer and the safe popped open. His shoulders slumped when he saw only one pistol and a box of ammunition.

"I was hoping for a shotgun or three."

"A 1911 .45 is pretty good. It will take down a man no problem."

His eyebrows shot to the top of his forehead.

"Hey, I grew up in Oklahoma."

He smiled and checked the gun, loaded a magazine, and pushed the gun into his belt. We both finished searching the house. When we met back up we smiled at each other, pleased at what we had found.

Of course that left us with our prisoner. He'd sat quietly while we ate and searched. I think he was just hoping we'd forget about him and disappear. But Tanner wasn't that dumb. He dragged the man and his chair to the middle of the living room where he could keep an eye on him. Then spread out a blanket on the couch and told me to find a room and crash.

Stifling a yawn, I was going to argue that we should share guard duties, but I was just too tired. Instead, I spent that night in a comfortable bed and wondered if this would be the last time I ever spent a night floating on a cloud.

As I lay there trying to sleep, I thought about our day. That morning we'd been running from a wave of water. I remembered how quickly Tanner had disarmed our prisoner. I swear, it was something to see.

I'd bent over hoping Tanner would understand. Hey, I'm woman enough to know what men think about. I just used my natural talents and let Tanner take care of the rest.

Then there had been the feeling of watching Tanner eat the food I'd made for him. I don't know. But it felt right, special.

Of course, I also thought about our future. What would we come up against? Would we make it? What was my brother doing? Ryan? Cassie? Had Uncle Frank gotten away? These and a thousand other worries danced through my brain until I finally fell asleep.

I was up early the next morning and had pancakes ready for when Tanner woke up. I knew he'd catnapped all night, waking up to check the prisoner then grabbing a quick nap before doing it all again.

Our prisoner looked like he'd experienced a hard night. I mean, he was old, maybe sixty. It must have been uncomfortable. But the man was alive. It beat the alternative.

Tanner wolfed down six large pancakes, half a plate of scrambled eggs, and two pieces of toast. I could only shake my head. The man could put away food. Something to remember. And not an ounce of fat on that body. I guess a man needs fuel if he's got muscles like that.

I made up a bunch of extra pancakes. Then stuffed dried noodles, a box of oatmeal, and salt and pepper shakers into my backpack.

"Okay," Tanner said as he started gathering our stuff. "I'll take this down to the boat, get the gas can and get the gas."

I could tell he wasn't looking forward to it.

When I heard him coming back up the trail, I stepped out the back and followed him to the garage. I knew I was leaving our prisoner, but I wanted to help. And no, I wasn't going to offer to siphon the gas. But I could be there for moral support.

Tanner cut a piece of garden hose and stuffed it into the gas tank. He then shot me a sad smile and started sucking.

Suddenly he choked and spit out a mouthful of gas, coughing and sputtering like our engine.

"God, I hate that," he said with a grimace as he wiped his mouth and continued to spit trying to get the taste out of his mouth.

My heart went out to him. But really, we didn't have a choice. "I'm going to have to do this every day until we get to Idaho," he said with a resigned look as he cracked a bottle of water and rinsed out his mouth.

Like I said, I wasn't going to offer to do it.

He then opened a bottle of motor oil and added it to the gas can. Seeing my confused expression he said, "Outboards need oil in the gas to keep things lubricated.

"How do you know stuff about boats?"

He shrugged as he tightened the cap. "Living in Oklahoma. You know about horses, right?"

His answer didn't really make sense. Was it a secret? His knowing about boats? Why?

For the first time, I was beginning to see that Tanner had more layers than he let show.

Something I needed to remember. The man wasn't just a collection of large muscles. No, there was more. The thought made me frown as my tummy twitched.

"What about our prisoner?" I asked, determined to shift my mind off the direction it had been headed.

Tanner shrugged. "We'll just leave him. He can smash the chair, get free, and find something to cut the ropes on his wrists."

I balked. It seemed too cruel. Seeing my doubt Tanner said, "If he found a weapon. Something we missed. He could shoot at us from the shore before we got away. I don't want to take the risk."

Nodding, I let out a long breath. He was right. I didn't like it, but he was right.

We never returned to the house. Tanner had moved everything to the boat. We got it running and we were back out on the river within minutes. This time, I didn't feel the same nervousness. Tanner had shown that he knew what he was doing. And really, this was so much better than walking.

We made good time. The shore was mostly trees interrupted by the occasional small town or beautiful mansions. The sun was out. But there were no planes. No other boats. And a weird silence. Oh sure, there was the occasional bird. The water slapped against the shore. Our engine. But nothing else. It was like we were the last leftover from human civilization.

Around lunch, four hours into our trip, Tanner turned the boat towards the shore. I shot him a questioning look. He pointed to the parkway and the dozen cars sitting on the road waiting to be siphoned off gas.

He pulled in, disconnected the can, grabbed the chunk of garden hose, and told me to stay with the boat, and raced up to a car. He was back in five minutes, sputtering, grimacing. But he didn't complain. Instead, he hooked everything back up and we were off.

It was getting late, we were just approaching Albany when he again pointed the boat towards the shore, the west bank this time.

I held my breath. We were coming into a city. Why here? Wouldn't it be better to stay in the forest? Then I thought about last nigh. No, forests could be just as dangerous as back alleys.

The wharves and piers looked intact, obviously, the wave hadn't reached this far north. But things still looked dead. A few people, but not many. Were they hiding? No, this was the industrial part of town. No power, no industry. No industry, no need for people.

Tanner suddenly put the boat in neutral and let us float as he lifted up to examine the shore. His brow narrowed until he found what he was looking for and started us into between two piers.

He worked us through the piling to ground the boat on a gravel beach in front of a warehouse.

"Stay here," he said as he put a hand on my shoulder to work past me and jump out onto the beach, he then dragged the boat up halfway out of the water and rushed up the beach and into a warehouse.

For the first time, I realized I was alone. I mean really alone. What would I do if he didn't come back? Yes, he'd left Jordan with me. And he'd never abandon Jordan. But what if something happened to him? I mean, Every time we tried to move forward there was something trying desperately to stop us. What would it be this time?

Gritting my teeth, my hand formed fists as I fought to not get up and race after him. I swear I was about to go when I saw him step out from between two buildings and wave for me to stay. As he slid down the beach towards us, he held up a hand to his lips.

"There are people, moving around. Raiding the building across the stress. Some of them are armed," he whispered. "I don't want to have to fight for a place to sleep so we'll crash over there, under the pier."

I looked where he was pointing and felt my stomach drop. A bare bench of earth, about four feet above the water, under the pier.

Not the most welcoming spot. But what choice did we have? We needed gas. And taking on people who didn't want to give up there gas was only going to end up with someone dead.

Chapter Nine

Tanner

I walked the boat along the edge of the water and then up under the pier. Haley watched me with a doubtful frown. I could see it in her eyes. The place had that unique smell of rotten water plants, fish, and creosote. I knew she was questioning my decision. But she hadn't seen the man being hit from behind and his wallet stolen.

No, we were better down here. And we couldn't go further upriver. The engine had been on fumes.

I doubled a blanket and spread it over the bare earth, then emptied our boat of our supplies before tying it off to one of the pilings.

Haley put on her peacoat and settled in.

"What's for dinner?" I asked.

I swear she was going to snap at me for assuming feeding me was her job because she was a girl. I just shot her a quick smile. Like I said before. Sometimes I just like to fight. I knew it wasn't her job. But pushing her buttons was fun.

"Pancakes," she said as she opened a plastic bag. "Dry ones."

Laughing, I accepted my share then leaned back against the concrete foundation and stared at the water slowly drifting by. An awkward silence fell over us. It was funny. We'd been in a boat all day but hadn't really talked.

"What do you think is going to happen," Haley suddenly asked as she brushed her hands together to clear the crumbs. "To people, the future?"

Wow, were did that come from? Shrugging, I said, "We're screwed. People. Civilization."

Her brow furrowed. "I agree, but why do you think so?"

Taking a deep breath I let it out slowly. I'd been thinking about this all day. "Before stuff like electricity, the combustion engine, chemical plants. Basic industry. Before that, the world's population was what? A billion? We're eight times bigger now. And we don't have the stuff that lets us get to so many people."

She sighed then nodded, obviously agreeing. "Not only that. But we don't know how to live in this world. I mean we don't have wood-burning stoves, stuff like that. Nor the knowledge or the tools are all gone."

The awkward silence returned as we both pondered what this future world was going to be like.

"How did you think about going upriver, the Erie Canal?"

I glanced over at her. Did she really think I was a clueless idiot? "Carry Simpson," I said as if that answered everything. When Haley frowned up at me I laughed and said. "She was shy, I wasn't. We were assigned a report in New York state history. She prepared the report. Told me what to say. It's probably the only thing I remembered from that class."

Haley nodded, "You didn't like school?"

Again I laughed. "Let's just say dislike is not extreme enough. More hated. Despised, Reviled."

She grinned. "Why. I mean I'm pretty sure you weren't bullied."

I paused as I wondered what to say then shrugged. "I'm dyslexic. Always have been."

She didn't frown, or pat my leg and say, 'you poor boy', I'll give her that. God how I hated talking about stuff like this, but she just seemed to pull it out of me.

"What about you?" I said, wanting to shift the focus off me.

I swear I could see in her eyes that she knew what I was doing and decided to let me off the personal stuff.

"I hoped to be going to Columbia next year."

"I'm not surprised," I said. "You've got college co-ed down."

Frowning, she said, "Art, design. Then hopefully a publishing house. I wanted to do book covers."

"You'll never get rich in publishing."

She scoffed, "None of us will ever get rich. Not now."

Again that awkward silence hit us as we were pulled back to our new reality.

Both of us sat there letting our minds wander. I made Jordan get on the other side of her. Haley's eyebrows rose in question.

"He'll keep you warm. Between the two of us, you should be toasty."

Suddenly her eyes grew as she realized we were going to be sleeping next to each other. The awkward silence jumped about twenty degrees.

"Why did you come?" she asked me suddenly. "I mean, you've got to admit. It is a big decision."

I paused for a second. I'd been asking myself the same question for the last two days. I could tell her it was because I knew the city was going to get bad. I could tell her that it was because she was pretty. But I'd known a dozen girls I could have shared some time with. But deep down. It was because I wanted the adventure. And this sounded like the ultimate adventure.

"Because," I said with a shrug.

Her brow furrowed showing me I'd pissed her off again. Like I said, I did enjoy pushing her buttons.

Rolling her eyes, she scooted down to go to sleep. I lay next to her, back-to-back, sharing three blankets. I could hear her breathing, feeling her back move with each breath. Okay, I'll admit my mind wandered to things I shouldn't be thinking about. Not with a girl like Haley. I knew the type. A good girl. A forever type girl.

Besides, we had a long trip in front of us. And my experience with long times and girls wasn't real good. I had a habit of pissing them off and them leaving. Haley wouldn't have that option. Not if she wanted to make Idaho.

The thought of her being stuck ate at my gut. So, I didn't try anything. No careless touches. No sweet words. No big bad man there to save her. It wasn't easy. In fact, it was probably one of the hardest nights of my life.

Sometime in the middle of the night I felt her move and realized I'd turned over and put my arm around her, holding her close. She gently lifted my arm and snuck out from beneath my embrace to hurry into the dark.

Jordan got up to go with her.

A few minutes later she climbed back under the blankets then snuggled back in next to me and pulled my arm back over her.

Gritting my teeth I forced my arm to remain were it was and eventually fell back asleep.

The morning had turned just gray enough to see the pier pilings. My back hurt from sleeping on the ground. But I held a beautiful girl in my arms, so life was pretty great.

She stirred, letting me know she was awake. But she didn't pull away. Was she pretending me holding her was no big deal? Maybe to her, it wasn't.

"I've got to go get the gas," I whispered as I turned away from her.

It only took me ten minutes. The people had disappeared after looting the warehouse. Windows were smashed and a car had been turned on its side. I ignored it and simply hit the next car and got our three gallons then rushed back to her.

A quick breakfast of bread and cheese then we loaded up the boat. Haley pushed us off and jumped it then smiled at me.

I tried to force the memory of holding her out of my mind and focused on getting us out of there.

The world seemed dead. Quiet. No cars. No lights, nothing but silent buildings. I guess rioters don't get up early in the morning. I wanted to get through Albany and start up the Mohawk river before they woke up.

We turned off the Hudson onto the smaller Mohawk but hit our first river lock in the first mile. The start of the Erie Canal. One of those modern locks. Big enough for grain barges. And worse, the gates were powered by a lockhouse. Electric.

"What now?" Haley asked with concern in her voice.

I simply shrugged, beached the boat just below the lock then carried our supplies to the other side, came back, shouldered the engine then dragged the boat up over a grassy bank and returned it to the river.

For the next three hours, we'd make a little progress then hit a lock and have to repeat our process. At the fourth, I stopped and said, "I've got to get some gas."

Haley nodded as she took a deep breath. I could see it in her eyes, people were coming out. When on the beach we were vulnerable. An old Lock Master watched me drag the boat then said, "We've got manual controls if we have to."

I laughed and said, "This is faster."

He rolled his eyes then shook his head. I was attaching the motor again when I called back at him. "Any camping stores around here?"

Frowning, he pointed to the small town. "About two blocks down. There's an Army surplus. They've got stuff. But this ain't the time to be camping. I swear, the world's crashing. Going to hell in a handbasket. Ain't got any news. The phones don't work. Ain't anyone know anything and you young people are out galivanting around like it's just another Tuesday."

I asked the old man to keep an eye on our stuff then grabbed the gas can, the hose, and the rifle and nodded for Haley and Jordan to come along. She frowned, I knew she had a dozen questions, but she bit her tongue.

The Army surplus store was crammed with things that suddenly looked very valuable. Camp stoves, tents, sleeping bags. And not just government-issue stuff, but name brands, probably seconds, but good enough.

"This place is going to be a gold mine in about two weeks when people run out of food and start heading for the hills."

Haley nodded, her eyes narrowed in concern. "How are you going to pay? The credit cards aren't going to work."

I ignored her and laid the rifle on the counter. The old guy behind the display case looked down at the rifle then up at me. I knew the type instantly, a bargainer, a born merchant. He raised an eyebrow, waiting for me to make the first move.

"I'm selling."

"You got the paperwork?"

I laughed, "The site isn't working. It was all on my computer and it isn't working either. But I don't think anyone is going to be doing background checks. Not any time soon."

He frowned, "This is New York state, son. They've got more rules about guns than my grandmother had about eating kosher. You can't sell a gun, and I can't buy one."

Taking a deep breath, I nodded as I laid the three bullets next to the rifle. "In a few days, this is going to be worth a ton. I mean a ton."

The man swallowed then nodded in agreement. I wondered how many people were wondering why they never purchased a weapon and where they could get one. I knew I was probably making a mistake getting rid of this rifle. But I knew I'd have difficulty finding ammunition. Besides, I still had the pistol.

"Listen," I said. "My friend," I pointed to Haley, "And I am going to grab two sleeping bags, a tent, and maybe some of that freeze-dried food. And anything else we can carry. In fact, my arms will be so loaded, I will probably forget all about the rifle and end up just leaving it."

The man looked down at the weapon then back at me as his mind swirled with possibilities. No paperwork. No cash. Then I think he began to figure it out. The rifle would come in handy, he didn't need another tent.

"Okay," he said as he snatched the rifle off the counter and hurried into the back.

I smiled at Haley then we spent the next ten minutes shopping, getting what we could. And good to my word. We only took what we could carry, but I've got big arms and can carry a lot.

We hit a car on the way back to the boat and loaded up with gas. Fifteen minutes later we were on the canal headed west.

Chapter Ten

Haley

Later that afternoon, I made a mistake. I laughed when Tanner struggled to put up the tent. It was obvious the boy had never been camping in his life. My brother, cousins, and I had gone a couple dozen times with my uncle.

Reaching out I offered to help. Tanner glared at me and said, "Don't you dare."

Okay, new lesson learned. Tanner did not like to be thought less of. Of course not. He was pure boy. Filled to the brim with competitive testosterone.

Careful, I said to myself. You might need that inner fury to be released. He'd done it with that man in the forest. My stomach clenched remembering how far we had to go and what we might run into.

Tanner eventually got the dome tent up then stood back with a satisfied smile.

"Do you think we can have a fire?" I asked. We'd stopped in a wooded part of the bank three miles past the last town.

He looked around then nodded.

I quickly gathered wood then got a small fire going. I moved some rocks and started a pot of water to boil. Once it was going, I dropped in two packs of stroganoff and sat back. Tanner had watched me intently, obviously learning how to start a campfire.

Wow, it was sort of strange being with someone who didn't know the basics. I mean, Tanner was so big, so competent, it was just weird, different. But he learned fast. Ryan, or Chase were experts in the forest. They could have lived off the land, hunting, fishing, wild plants. Tanner not so much. He might know everything about surviving in New York City. But that wasn't going to be valuable anymore.

That became our routine. Camping, scrounging for gas, portaging our stuff around the locks. Avoiding people. Surviving.

When we hit the outskirts of Buffalo my insides tightened. We were entering unknown territory. The power had been out for a week. It was easy to imagine people starting to freak as they saw the end fast approaching.

How much food did people have in their homes? What happened when it all disappeared? Twice we saw smoke rising from deep in the city. Fires that people couldn't put out.

A couple approached us in a canoe, headed down river. Tanner maneuvered the boat to give them room. The woman in the bow smiled as she dipped her oar. The guy in the back ignored us. Tanner suddenly cut the engine into neutral letting the boat come to a natural stop near the canoe.

"It's clear all the way to Manhattan," Tanner said to them, obviously hoping for information.

The man frowned then shrugged, "it's clear to Lake Erie."

"Where you headed?" Tanner asked.

The woman turned back to look at her partner then said, "Away. The city ... things are going from bad to worse."

"What do you mean?" I asked as my stomach clenched. Would we get through?

She frowned then shuddered. "People are going crazy. Gangs are taking whatever they want. People are getting shot and just left in the streets. The government ... there is no government."

I glanced back at Tanner, silently asking if we should try getting through. He of course ignored me and asked the couple. "Have you heard any news, out west?"

The man scoffed and shook his head. "How? Nothing works. No radios, no internet, Nothing but rumors, each more wrong than the last."

"We're headed to Idaho," I suddenly said. "Down the Ohio then up the Missouri."

The couple blanched, unable to fathom such a journey. "I thought us trying for Vermont was risky. But Idaho, you're crazy."

A feeling of certainty filled me. The man was probably right.

"Well, good luck," Tanner said with a wave as he dropped the boat back into gear. The couple waved back and wished us luck then dipped their oars and headed east while we continued west. Two boats passing. People sharing a moment then never coming together again.

I looked back at Tanner and almost cried. Were we doing the right thing? How could we think we would make it all the way to Idaho? It had only been a week and we hadn't even gotten out of New York state. And from what those people said, things were only going to get worse.

As we passed through the city my stomach tumbled with worry. Everything was so quiet, people were out, some looking, others walking around in a bit of a daze. They would stare at us as we passed with a hint of jealousy in their eyes.

I pushed the worry down and focused on helping Tanner navigate, pointing out anything floating in the canal. Twice we had to pull over and work our way around the locks. Tanner handed me the pistol and told me to stay with our stuff until he returned.

Swallowing I held the pistol with both hands, praying I wouldn't have to use it.

Tanner tied Jordan next to our stuff on the other end and returned. He had to make two trips then grabbed the boat and dragged it to the other side of the lock.

I sighed heavily when we started out again, wondering what was going to happen to all these people. Tanner didn't seem phased at the thought of all the future suffering. I swear, it was like he had put them all out of his mind. How could he not see what was going to happen to them? I thought back to the men on the road before the wave washed over them.

How many would die in the next few months? Billions, I thought.

When we hit Lake Erie, I gasped. It was so big. We'd been cramped on both sides. But this was open water. How would our little boat ever make it?

"I'll stay close to the beach," Tanner said as he turned the boat south.

A small chop rocked the boat making my stomach queasy. Jordan whined and I knew he was feeling the same sea sickness.

Tanner ignored it, determined to move us forward. Ever forward.

Suddenly, Tanner made a sharp turn and pointed to a breakwater and a marina.

I shot him a questioning look. "We walk from here until we catch the Ohio River."

Saying goodbye to the boat was sort of hard. We'd been so attached, our very lives depended upon it. And now we were just going to walk away. It seemed wrong. But Tanner tied it off at the first wharf and unloaded our stuff.

He swung the backpack over his shoulders then shot me a quick look asking why I was taking so long.

I quickly scrambled into my pack. We'd prepared last night. His was bigger, with the tent tied off below and his sleeping bag on top. The blankets and my Peacoat were tied off on the top of mine.

"We need to find a place for the night," he called back as his boots echoed off the wooden planks.

I let out a long breath. So much for sentimentality. We were starting a new phase of our journey. But Tanner could care less. No big deal. I could only shake my head. The guy was as cold as a stone.

We worked our way out of the marina and up onto a road, headed south. How far, I wondered? And what would we run into along the way? A new nervousness filled me. We were around people again. We could be attacked easily. The safety and security of the canal seemed so far behind us. Really, his plan had been smart. We were farther along than if we had walked. We had avoided major conflicts.

No, things were going good I reminded myself, determined to see the positive.

Of course, that thought lasted about half an hour.

We were rounding a corner when we came upon a man and woman fighting in the middle of the street. He was pulling at her arm. She was punching at him, trying to break free.

"Hey," Tanner yelled as he dropped his pack and raced towards the couple.

My heart stopped. Tanner was rushing into danger without knowing what was going on.

The man whipped around without letting go of the woman's arm. Seeing a small giant racing towards him, he blanched, then dropped the woman's arm and pulled a gun from his belt, and fired.

No warning, no discussion. Just a quick shot.

I dropped to the ground, pulling my pack in front of me for cover. Tanner, being Tanner, didn't even stop, he pulled his own weapon, but before he could fire a bullet hit him, twisting him sideways.

My stomach clenched as I watched in slow motion. Tanner gathered himself, then took aim, and fired hitting the man in the chest.

The man fell back, firing over and over as he twisted and dropped face-first.

"Tanner," I yelled as I rushed toward him.

He waved me back and called, "I'm okay," over his shoulder as he slowly advanced on the man, his pistol covering him expecting him to come back to life.

I held my breath, unable to believe what had just happened. A week of nothing, then suddenly my world exploded with gunfire. I was watching Tanner watch the man when the woman groaned and slumped to the ground.

She held her stomach as blood poured out from between her fingers. The look of fear in her eyes would sit with me for the rest of my life. The man's wild firing had hit her.

Racing to her I gently helped her down. Tanner continued to cover the man then kicked him in the foot to get a reaction. I was busy covering the woman's hands. Frantically trying to figure out what to do.

The woman looked up at me, suddenly a calmness washed over her. "My baby," she said then glanced at the sidewalk.

My heart lurched when I saw a baby wrapped in a pink parka lying on the sidewalk, next to a baby bag, staring at the world, wondering what was going on.

"No," I gasped as the reality of the situation hit me. It was so wrong to see a small baby like that, lying on the concrete. Almost a sacrilege.

"Her name is Britney, Britney Jean Carson," the woman whispered as she grabbed my hand in a death grip. "The man, he came out of nowhere."

I thought of the alley and the two men who had tried to take me.

"Save her," the woman whispered.

"You'll be okay," I said with false comfort.

The woman started to laugh then coughed. A trickle of blood leaked from the corner of her mouth making me even more terrified. The woman was dying right in front of me.

Tanner knelt down next to me and looked into the woman's eyes. "Where should we take her? Family?"

My god, was he admitting the woman was going to die? No, he couldn't do that. She needed hope. How dare he?

The woman took a deep breath then shook her head. "There's no one. You. You have to save her."

Tanner and I looked at each other, the woman had realized she wasn't going to live.

"We'll get her to the authorities."

"NO!" the woman croaked as she grabbed my hand and pulled be close. "You. It has to be you."

My heart stopped. No, this was impossible.

"Promise me," she said, staring into my eyes, then at Tanner. "Promise. I have to know it will be you."

Neither of us could make that promise, we just stared back at her, unable to speak.

She grimaced through the pain then said. "The city. No authorities. She'd die. It has to be you."

The woman then started grimacing before coughing one more time.

"We promise," Tanner suddenly said as he gently pushed the hair out of her eyes.

The woman smiled up at him then slumped into death, her eyes staring at the sky.

I froze, unable to believe what had just happened. "Tanner, we can't take a baby."

He frowned at me. "I just wanted to make her easy. To rest her soul. But she's right. Who's going to take on a baby now? Feed her, care for her. Before this is over, people will be burying their own kids."

"But ..."

He took a deep breath then looked at me. "It's your choice. We can take her with us. Or we can try to find someone to take her off our hands. We don't have to decide right now. Maybe we will find someone along the way. In the meantime. I want to get out of here. I just killed a man. He might have brothers. Friends."

A wave of hopelessness washed over me. Ten minutes earlier we had been walking down a road. Now we were responsible for a baby. Suddenly, his words hit me. He'd killed a man. What did he feel? Was he torn up inside, or was he casually dismissive? Which would be worse, I wondered?

Suddenly, the baby began to cry, and I felt my world shift as a great weight settled on my shoulders, and a strange need burned inside of me.

Chapter Eleven

Tanner

My world was whirling, spinning down a drain. We'd gone from a beautiful day to pure hell in an instant. Glancing down I winced at the tear in my arm. Things worked, so the bullet hadn't hit a bone. Just torn a strip out of my upper right arm.

Great, the slice on my left arm was almost healed, or at least not bleeding, and now I had a chunk missing on my right. At this rate, I'd have enough holes to make a calendar before we got to Idaho.

Haley was holding the baby, rocking her back and forth, whispering to her, trying to get her to stop crying. My heart broke. The world sucked, but a baby shouldn't have to go through this.

Turning, I glanced back at the man laying in the middle of the street. It took every bit of self-control to stop myself from kicking him. God, I wished I could bring him back to life just so I could kill him again. He'd ruined a little baby's life. Why?

Then a heavy guilt hit me. If I hadn't charged, the woman would still be alive. The baby would still have a mother. No, I tried to tell myself. This wasn't my fault. But deep down, I knew it was. Once again, my bull-in-a-China shop attitude had hurt someone.

Haley looked at me, her eyes torn with misery and confusion. She then saw my wound and gasped. "You're hurt."

"I'll be fine," I said as I went back and grabbed my pack. My arm screamed in pain as I worked the backpack up onto my shoulders. I'd take care of it later. We needed to get out of there. I really was worried about other people. Friends of the man showing up.

In fact, I was surprised we weren't surrounded by a dozen angry neighbors. Six or seven shots erupting on their street should have raised some concerns. But obviously, people were too afraid to get involved. And there was no 911 to call.

I pried the gun out of the man's hand, gritted my teeth, and rifled through his pockets for any ammunition, coming up empty. I then grabbed Haley's pack and said, "We need to go."

Her eyes widened then she looked at the woman, "What about ..."

"We don't have time to bury her."

Haley's jaw dropped in surprise. "But ... We can't just leave her."

"Haley, we have to go. Now," I said as I gently lifted the diaper bag then took her arm and started her up the street. Every alarm was sounding off at full blast. I held a pack in one hand, a diaper bag in the other. Someone was going to come, and I'd be slower than a snail. I'd end up dead, or worse, Haley and the baby would be hurt.

She balked for a second, obviously devastated, then she looked down at the baby and something changed in her eyes. Acceptance. I could read it easily. A week together and I was getting to where I could tell what she was thinking by just a look. The baby. That was what was important. More than anything. We needed to stay alive to save the baby.

Taking a deep breath, she nodded then allowed me to lead her out of there.

"We'll find some place to hole up," I said as I shifted to keep myself slightly in front of her and the baby.

Jordan kept back next to Haley, looking up at her and the baby, obviously concerned.

It was two blocks before I could allow myself to begin to relax. We were out of the kill zone. I continued to scan the area for any threat, but I was able to go back over what had happened. Obviously, the man had tried to take the woman. She'd been able to put the baby down to begin to fight. I'd come along and ruined everything.

A guilt ate at my soul, but I pushed it aside. I'd deal with it later. I just needed to get Haley and the baby to safety. Some place we could hide and lick our wounds.

Somewhere along the way, the baby stopped crying letting Haley sigh with relief.

We were halfway through the town when I spotted what I needed. A warehouse between two brick buildings. Dark windows. No noises, no people.

"There," I said as I hurried Haley across the street. I paused to make sure no one was watching then kicked the door open. For a split second, I froze waiting to be attacked. But nothing. Sticking my head in, I checked it out and sighed. It'd work.

Stepping in, I turned and pulled Haley into the building then slammed the door shut. I had to use a splintered two-by-four to hold the door closed. Just enough light leaked in from the windows to show us an empty room. Bare concrete floor. Metal walls. Steel stanchions holding up the roof. I wondered about what the place had been used for then said a quick thanks that there hadn't been anything in here worth looting.

Haley held the baby to her chest, rocking back and forth as she looked around then back at me.

"There," I said as I pointed to an office in the far corner. A small ten-foot by ten-foot office with windows overlooking the warehouse floor.

Jordan quickly explored the bare office, sniffing, learning who and what had been there over the last ten years.

I dropped my stuff then squirmed out of my pack and let out a long sigh.

Haley twisted looking around then back at me. "What now?"

"We hide, until dark. Then sneak out of town."

She looked down at the baby then whimpered. "We can't just take the baby. That's kidnapping."

I started to shrug then winced when my arm screamed in protest. Sighing, I began to use my left hand to unbutton my shirt.

Haley watched me for a second then said, "Let me get the baby settled then I'll fix your arm." She laid out all our blankets, found the little girl a toy unicorn in the diaper bag, and set her down, covering her with a throw quilt her mom had probably made for her.

My heart broke. The little girl would never know her mother. Never know the woman who had fought to keep her alive.

"Here," Haley said as she lit a candle then pulled my shirt from my jeans before gingerly working it up and off my shoulders.

I smiled. I'd always imagined being undressed by Haley in slightly different circumstances. She saw the glint in my eye and frowned at me. "Get your mind out of the gutter."

Laughing, I felt myself relax and let her take over.

She grabbed the first aid stuff from her pack then started probing and prodding the wound. It was about three inches long. More of a gash.

"Just as the wound on your left arm was all healed. Now this,"

I smiled. "You're getting to be an expert."

"It would be okay with me if I never have to do this again. Just so you know."

Suddenly she smeared some goop all over the wound making me wince and pull away. "You enjoy doing that."

She smiled up at me and said, "No I don't. Not really. But you're so big. I figured you could handle it."

I leaned back against the wall as she worked and closed my eyes. The day's events playing over and over. But they were slowly pushed aside by the scent of Haley, that unique lavender smell mixed with medicine and her soft touch as she tried to heal me.

A man could become lost I thought as I allowed a calmness to fill me.

Weird, I thought. Normally after a fight, it took hours for me to come down. But one gentle touch by this girl and I was filled with a calmness.

Suddenly the baby whimpered pulling her attention away from me. And no, I didn't feel a pang of jealousy. At least not much of one.

Haley finished wrapping a bandage around my arm then hurried back to scoop up the baby. "I think she's hungry,"

"How can you tell," I asked. I mean, it was a baby.

She shot me a look that was pure woman. It was obvious to her. Scrambling through the diaper bag she found a large can of powdered formula and let out a heavy sigh. Next, she found bottled water and baby bottles.

She quickly made a bottle and held the baby as she fed her. "It should be heated," she said about the bottle. "But she doesn't mind."

I couldn't help but smile. The baby was lucky. If it had been up to me, I'd have been lost. "You're good at that," I said to her.

She smiled back then turned away to continue rocking the baby.

I closed my eyes and tried to ignore the pain in my arm. What now? How were we supposed to get to Idaho with a baby?

Just do it, I thought to myself. One step in front of the other. At night, I thought. That would be our best chance. Sneaking away before anyone even knew we were there.

Haley finished feeding the baby then changed her diaper, swaddled her in blankets and laid her down then scooted over to sit next to me.

I looked down and saw the fear in her eyes. A fear mixed with a determination.

"We need stuff," she said. "Formula, diapers, baby food. I saw some jars. I think she was starting to shift over to regular food."

I nodded, pretending I knew what she was talking about.

She was silent for a long moment then said. "This is ridiculous. We can't just take a baby."

I didn't answer, letting her come to the realization that we didn't have a choice. "I'm open to suggestions. But I think we're her best bet."

Haley looked up at me with doubt in her eyes.

"Believe me. The easy thing would be to dump her on someone else. Anyone else? But … but I sort of feel we owe it to her. At least I do. If I hadn't charged that guy. Her mother would still be alive."

Haley stared up at me, her eyes searching mine. "You can't feel guilty. You did the right thing."

Shrugging, I glanced over at the baby and said, "Maybe, but that doesn't change the fact.

She's our responsibility. Not only because of what I did. But we promised her mom."

"I don't know," Haley said as she stared at the sleeping baby.

"Think about it, Haley. You said yourself. Where would be better than a farm in Idaho for a little girl to grow up? Here in a city? No way. The food is going to run out in the next week or so. It's the middle of spring. Have you seen anyone preparing, putting in gardens? No. they're still in denial. Still waiting for the government to come save them."

She thought for a long moment then sighed heavily. "Okay. But if we find somewhere for her. We have to do what is best for her."

I nodded. "Sure. Like I said, I'm not looking forward to taking a baby across the country. If we find somewhere for her. Believe me, I'll jump at the chance."

Letting out a long breath she then asked, "So what next?"

"We sneak out, tonight, after dark. We should have enough for a few days. Then we find the stuff we need."

She nodded then leaned her head on my good shoulder and sighed.

Without thinking, I shifted to put my arm around her. My heart ached at seeing her worried and scared. Not for herself, but for the little baby laying on our blankets.

The soft burble of the baby woke us. She was laying on her back staring up at the ceiling, the soft candlelight bathing the room in a yellow light.

"We need to be going," I said as I pushed up off the wall and winced. My arm had tightened up. It was going to be a long night. "I'll take your pack. You take the bag and the baby."

"Her name is Britney," Haley said as she gently scooped her up and snuggled her neck, taking in her scent.

Wincing, I shouldered my pack, adjusted the two guns in my belt, then lifted Haley's pack. She stuffed the blankets over the top of the diaper bag while rocking the baby. I gingerly led us out of the warehouse into a dark that made me hesitate. There was a quarter moon and a cloudy sky. And worse, dark buildings lining he street.

So weird.

I led us out to the middle of the street to give me more time to react in case anyone came for us. It took me a few minutes to find the main road that headed south. How far? I wondered. We needed to find the river.

The town was strange, quiet, black, lurking danger. But the countryside was worse. We left the town and entered forested rolling hills that hid a thousand terrors. I constantly scanned the trees expecting a monster to jump out at any minute.

So different than home. There I had known what terrors lurked in the shadows. I'd run across them a thousand times. Junkies looking for a quick fix. Monsters looking for an easy score or kids to use. But this was different. Out here, there was no telling.

Haley stopped to pull a blanket and drape it over her, and the baby then nodded for me to continue.

It was only when we'd gone about five miles that I began to relax. One, no friends or relatives of the man I'd killed. No werewolves or vampires. Just a quite night walking down a road. Of course that all changed when I saw a fire flickering in the distance. Figures walking around the fire, laughing, and cursing.

I held up my hand to stop Haley. I was trying to figure if we could sneak by or maybe take a detour around the fire. Of course, at that exact moment the baby decided she didn't like stopping and began to cry.

A man said, "hush." The people around the fire suddenly scrambled.

I pushed Haley into the forest next to us, but Britney continued to whimper and cry, announcing our position to every monster within a ten-mile radius.

Chapter Twelve

Haley

"Hush," I whispered to Britney as I wrapped my hand around her head to protect her as we raced through the trees. Branches poked at me while I fought to get away from the people chasing us.

Suddenly, Tanner jumped in front of me breaking through the branches, clearing a path. I tucked in behind him, cradling Britney, praying we could get away.

Behind us, a half dozen men called out to each other, some holding burning torches, others flashlights, searching for their prey.

My heart pounded as I was pulled back to thinking about being dragged into that alley. That thought was followed by the memory of Tanner having to kill the man attacking Britney's mom. Were these people friends of his? Had they somehow gotten in front of us, waiting to take their revenge?

Tanner cursed under his breath, reached out, and held a branch back for me to pass through then once again charged in front. Britney whimpered at first then stopped crying. What was it about this girl? As long as we were moving, she was perfectly happy.

"Here," Tanner said as he held out his hand to help me jump over a ditch. I grabbed it, letting him pull me over then grabbed his belt to make sure we didn't get separated in the dark. He continued working through the forest. Just enough weak silver moonlight seeped through the canopy to let him pick a path.

He slammed to a halt so quickly I banged into his backpack.

"A road," he whispered as he stepped aside for me to see asphalt in both directions. "This way," he added, pushing me south. Now he fell back, protecting me from behind. For just the briefest moment I feared he was going to stay behind. Take on these men to give me time to get away. I mean, he was the kind of guy who could do something that idiotic. Didn't he realize I'd never make it without him? Not with the baby.

But, he didn't stay behind, instead catching up and gently pushing at my lower back to keep me going.

Suddenly, the men broke out of the forest about a hundred yards behind us. Tanner grabbed my shoulder, "Freeze," he whispered.

My stomach fell as I bounced Britney, terrified she'd start crying.

We stayed there locked in position, afraid to move, hoping that we were too far away for the torchlight to spot us.

When glass shattered, someone cussed and said, "Be careful Jimmy, that stuff doesn't grow on trees."

Someone laughed, the others grumbled, upset they'd lost us. "To hell with them," someone said then turned back to the forest. Someone said something about not giving up, but the others simply said it wasn't worth it. Eventually, there was a lone man on the road, shining his flashlight first south, then north, then south, searching for us.

I held my breath, terrified Britney would cry out. Please go away, I prayed in my mind over and over. I didn't want anyone else dying today. Tanner would beat himself up about it.

When the man turned north, Tanner let out a long breath, held a finger to his lips, and urged me forward. "Slow," he whispered.

We quietly started down the road, me rocking Britney, Tanner watching the forest and the road behind us. When the man's flashlight disappeared, I was finally able to let out a long breath of relief.

Tanner shot me a quick smile that I could barely see in the darkness.

"How's the baby?" he asked.

"Britney is asleep," I said as I rolled my eyes. "I swear, she only relaxes when the world is ending."

He laughed, "She's going to be the most relaxed baby in history before this is over."

My stomach clenched tight as I realized just how right he was. How could we think of taking a baby to Iowa? I mean, how could we think we could take a baby anywhere? What gave us the right? We were risking her life. The last few minutes proved that.

No, I realized. We had to find somewhere for her.

"The next town," I said to Tanner, "We have to find someone. Child services, the police. Someone."

He glanced over at me then let his shoulders slump as he nodded.

My soul rested, it was the right thing. But a worry gnawed at my gut. How could I let someone else take her? It was so strange, this new bond I had with her. It had hit me the first time I'd picked her up. This need to care and protect. To make her world perfect.

It was so terrible, the way her life was starting out. So unfair. The world ending, her mom dying, so darn unfair. Every part of me cried out to end it, the unfairness.

Taking a deep breath, I gently moved the blanket so I could look down at her and felt my heart melt. She was so perfect. A chubby little face, long eyelashes. Leaning down I took a deep breath to soak in her smell of talcum powder, dried milk, and all baby.

God, I was going to break into a thousand pieces when I had to give her away.

Gritting my teeth, I pushed the tears away and focused on walking ahead. We needed to get to the next town. I feared it, but we had to.

The sky was turning gray a couple of hours later. Light enough to where I could see the forest. "Here," I said as I dropped her bag and tried to hand Britney to Tanner.

He yelped and backed up two steps, holding his hands up like I'd tried to hand him a live hand grenade. I almost laughed, the look of pure fear in his eyes was priceless.

"Just hold her," I snapped. I didn't have time for him to be squeamish, the bushes had been calling for me for the last hour.

He took a deep breath and allowed me to give him Britney. He used both hands, holding her out away from his body as if she might contaminate him. I swear it was almost cute.

"Like this," I said as I showed him how to tuck her into the crook of his arm. "Like a football."

He frowned at me but then he looked down at the baby and almost smiled. Wow, I thought. She was with Tanner for ten seconds and he smiled. I'd seen only one or two in the last week.

When I came back from the forest, I found him staring down, tickling her chin, and the baby giggling like she'd found the greatest toy in the history of the world. I swear there was a hint of jealousy, but I'm human.

Tanner saw me and quickly shut down, refusing to admit he'd enjoyed taking care of her, and let out a long sigh when I took her from him. Grabbing the diaper bag, I started down the road, determined to get to the next town.

The sun had just come up when we hit Providence Ohio, population 12,398. "Big enough to have services," Tanner said.

"Small enough to care," I answered as my heart ached. No, I kept reminding myself this was the right thing. There had to be someone better qualified, better able to care for her.

Tanner moved in front of me as we entered the town, shifting my pack to his left hand so that he could grab his gun with his right. I was learning about my tame monster. I knew what he was doing and why and my heart was thankful. There were none of these silly ideas bout women's lib. I needed a man to take the slings and arrows. Especially now with the baby.

People were out and about. Some glanced at us as we walked down the middle of the road. Cars were parked along the sidewalk. Others still sat in the middle of the road. The businesses were dark, but the windows hadn't been broken.

A woman walked from behind a building her arms loaded with cardboard. I frowned until I realized she was scrambling for something to burn so she could cook her family breakfast.

Wow, a thousand yards from a forest full of trees and she was going to use cardboard.

People just do what they know, I realized and felt a twinge of worry. They were going to have to adapt, or they wouldn't survive.

"There," he said, pointing to a police station with a flag blowing in the breeze.

My heart hitched and I almost stumbled, suddenly terrified of losing Britney. I almost told him to stop, that I'd changed my mind, but I thought about my Uncle Frank telling me that doing what was right always worked out the best in the long run.

Taking a deep breath, I walked with Tanner to the police station. He pulled the door open and stepped aside to let me go first.

A policeman looked up from a desk covered in stacks of papers. An oil lamp burned on the corner of the desk throwing the room into a weak yellow light. The cop's eyes narrowed when he saw us.

My heart hammered in my chest as I looked around, hoping maybe there was a lady cop who would understand. But the place was empty. The offices were behind a glass window. There was just enough light to see this guy was all alone.

"We found a baby," Tanner said.

God, I wanted to slap his arm. Could he be any more blunt?

The cop's gaze narrowed as he looked at little Britney then back up at Tanner. "So?"

Both Tanner and I froze. Neither of us had expected that.

The cop shook his head. "Everything has gone to crap. You finding a baby is about problem eight hundred thirty-two on my list."

He started moving forms from one pile to another then looked up at us, surprised to see us still there.

"What should we do with her," Tanner asked.

The cop let out a long sigh then slumped in defeat. I thought for a second, he was going to offer to take her, and I felt myself stiffen in resistance. This guy wasn't qualified to care for a puppy, let alone a six-month-old baby.

"Take her to City Hall, two blocks south, over one," he glanced over at the clock. "There might be someone there by now, but maybe not."

A stomach knot made me worry the guy was just shuffling us off to someone else. Tanner frowned as he studied the guy then shrugged at me and nodded to the door.

When we stepped outside Tanner shook his head. "The guy is more worried about his paperwork than the world ending."

"Why was he the only one there?"

Tanner scoffed, "He might be the only one left. Maybe the others are at home, taking care of their families."

A nervousness began to fill me as we worked our way to the city hall. Fortunately, this time we found a woman. A nice older woman with a name tag, Alice Jenson, it said. Her eyes lit up when she saw us come through the door. My insides relaxed the woman had experienced grandmother written all over her. The sensible dress, the hair in a bun, glasses on a chain around her neck.

Bureaucrat and grandmother, the perfect match, just what we needed.

"We found a baby," Tanner said with his new favorite line.

The woman smiled up at him then looked at the baby.

"Her mother is dead," I added hoping she'd understand why we'd taken the baby. That we weren't kidnappers.

The woman sighed then held out her hands for little Britney. "Oh, aren't you a doll," she said as she kissed her cheek.

My heart broke as Briteny smiled up at the woman. "Her name is Britney Jean Carson," I said. "Her mom told us before she died."

The woman just nodded. My stomach clenched, she didn't even write it down. She wasn't asking a dozen questions, wasn't filling out forms. Instead, she just kept looking down at the baby.

"What's going to happen to her," Tanner asked. His brow was furrowed, and I was seeing that hint of fight beginning to build inside of him. I was learning, that look meant he was on guard, ready to attack.

The hair on Jordan's neck stood up as he moved in next to Tanner. Even the dog could feel the tension.

The woman, Mrs. Freemont finally looked away from the baby then back at us and shrugged. "I don't know. I mean, I can't get a hold of the state service people. I guess I could take her to the hospital. Or I could just take her home with me."

Without warning, Tanner reached over and pulled Britney from the woman's arms. She shot him a frown.

"If you don't know what to do. I guess we'll take her to her aunt's. She is supposed to live in the next town."

The old woman frowned, obviously not believing him. She kept glancing at the baby in his arms, then up at him.

"You can't do that," she said with her sternest expression.

Tanner laughed, "Who's going to stop us?" Then he turned and marched out of the building, grabbing both packs with one hand, grunting at their weight then looking over his shoulder, silently asking me why I wasn't coming.

My heart burst with happiness. I wasn't going to lose Britney.

"What are you doing?" I asked.

Tanner shot me a quick frown. "She's better off with us." A simple statement with which I agreed wholeheartedly.

I mean, how hard could it be to walk across a continent with a baby? Besides. She was our responsibility now and my heart knew it was the right thing.

Chapter Thirteen

Tanner

As we hurried down the street I glanced over at Haley and the baby and shuddered. What was I doing? How could I think I was going to get them to safety? My gut tightened. Ten days ago I had been all alone, free. Now I was responsible for a pretty girl and a baby. Oh yeah, and the world was ending.

I knew what we were going to face. The monsters had been set free. No authorities to run to. No civilization to rely upon. Sure, there was some semblance. It hadn't sunk in yet. But it was coming, I could feel it in every fiber of my being. Things were going to get so much worse.

"We need to find supplies," I said.

Haley nodded. I could see in her eyes that she still wasn't sure we were doing the right thing. And I sort of agreed with her. But what choice did we have?

"A hospital," I said, "A maternity ward. They might have what we need. Stores aren't going to give us formula and diapers."

Again, Haley nodded. "You're probably right."

A silence fell over us as we continued out of town. No one chased us. No flashing lights, no sirens. Just the occasional person watching us walk by each lost in their own bit of hell. Each worried about their own future and not wanting to take on more problems.

Then it hit me. They saw us as a family. A young couple with their baby. A team. Not three separate individuals thrown together by circumstances. A new fear filled me as I thought about Haley. Did she see it? This new dynamic.

"We also need food," she added.

I nodded. "And a place to crash. But let's wait until we get to the next town."

The silence returned. Both of us focused on getting down the road. The morning sky had become gray as a storm began to form on the horizon. We were going to get hit by rain later that afternoon would have been my guess.

We were almost out of town when I saw a blue sign with a large H indicating the way to a hospital. I glanced over at Haley, raising an eyebrow.

She nodded and followed me as we turned off the main road. The hospital was a three-story building, glass, and steel. My heart fell when I realized the windows were dark. But it was the silence that hit me. No emergency generators. God, I wouldn't want to be in the middle of open-heart surgery when the lights went out. I wondered how many people died on the operating table throughout the country.

Gritting my teeth I made Haley walk behind me as we approached. When we got to the front door, I dropped out gear and tied off Jordan to guard it. He frowned at me, obviously not liking the idea of being left behind.

An old man holding the arm of a frail older woman approached the glass door in front of us. I rushed forward to push the door open for them.

The older woman smiled at me then balked when she saw the darkness inside. Enough light got in from all the windows, but the place still didn't feel right. There was a stale smell different than the normal hospital smell. More dust, less cleanser. People were mingling about, some holding injured limbs. Other's moaning in chairs rocking back and forth.

A harried nurse was working her way through the crowd, writing on a clipboard then hurrying to the next patient, feeling foreheads, peeling blankets back to look at wounds then moving on.

She glanced up and immediately focused on the baby. "Pediatrics," she said. "Down the hall, to the right." She then turned to the older couple and started asking questions.

I touched Haley's lower back to start her down the dark hall. A cold chill ran down my spine. These people were sick, and I didn't want to let the baby near them. There was no telling what they might have.

The hall was long and gray, lit only by the windows on either end. We found the pediatric department next to the maternity ward. My heart fell when I saw a boy about eight holding his obviously broken arm. A soon-to-be mother sat with her swollen belly, looking as if her world was coming to an end, repeatedly looking at the doors that led into the maternity ward.

"Yes?" A nurse behind a desk asked us, she looked harried, like the last thing she needed was another patient. How were they doing this? I mean, all of modern medicine had been tossed out the window. No ultrasounds, no monitors. Storm lanterns and stethoscopes. They'd been thrown back a hundred years, but they were still trying.

"We found ..."

Haley put a hand on my arm, stopping me. "We need formula," she said, "And diapers. The stores are all closed."

The woman frowned for a second then laughed. A sad, almost insane laugh. "I've got a leukemia patient and no more medicine. A boy with a broken arm and no anesthesia to set it, let alone any X-rays. The insulin is going bad because our refrigerators don't work. And a family at home wondering why their mother isn't with them as the world comes apart."

My insides shifted, suddenly my problems didn't seem so terrible. But the woman smiled. "Finally, a problem I can solve."

I held my breath, it was impossible to think we might actually catch a break.

"Come with me," she said as she waved us back. Haley and I followed her through the double doors to the ward where she opened a locker and started pulling out three large cans of powdered formula. "This will last you about a month, six weeks. More if supplemented with soft foods."

She smiled at the baby who stared at her with big eyes, obviously melting the woman's heart. She then smiled at Haley, "You're a good mom. She looks healthy. Happy almost."

I swear Haley's eyes almost teared up. No better words had ever been spoken.

The woman then opened another locker and removed a large pack of diapers. Then smiled and handed us a pack of cloth diapers. "These for when you run out." She then started handing over tubes of gel. Two different pacifiers, and packs of diaper wipes. It was like hitting the lottery.

"How can we pay for this?" I asked as a new worry hit me.

She just shook her head. "They're samples. The companies give them to us to hand out hoping you'll get hooked on their product."

My arms were loaded as I tried to balance everything. Suddenly I felt a warmth fill me. Not everyone was going crazy. Not everyone was becoming an instant monster. There were still good people on this earth.

"Thank you," Haley said as she gave the woman a quick hug.

The nurse smiled back at her then tickled the baby's cheek. "You two just love your baby."

I had to bite back an instant reaction to correct her. Instead, I glanced at Haley and nodded to the door. We needed to get out of there before these people discovered the baby wasn't ours.

When we got outside, I pulled Haley aside and started loading up the diaper bag and backpacks. I swear it was like we'd hit the mother load.

Haley rocked the baby, whispering to her then she looked up at me and I saw a sadness in her eyes that hit me.

"What if she gets sick," Haley said. "What if we run out of antibiotics? What if she gets hurt?"

I tightness in my gut made me take a deep breath. "We do the best we can."

Haley looked at me obviously upset. Our best might not be good enough.

I shouldered my pack, picked up Haley's pack then the diaper bag, and started out of town with Jordan jogging next to us. Haley carried the baby, hurrying to keep up with me. I felt a need to be gone. We had been lucky. Lucker than we deserved. That obviously meant things were going to go bad. It was the way things were now. Good must always be outweighed by ten bads.

We left town and I felt the weight of the days catch up with me. We'd been walking all night, and I was carrying Ninety pounds. I'm a big guy but even I can get tired. Suddenly Haley pointed to a dark house set back from the road.

I frowned for a moment wondering what she was seeing then it hit me. The place was empty. Dark windows didn't mean anything, but long grass that hadn't been cut in months. A dozen newspapers folded up sitting on the front step where the paperboy had tossed them. Mail sticking out of a full mailbox.

Haley looked at me, questioningly. I sighed and nodded. "It's worth checking out." My shoulders hunched as I motioned for her and the baby to hold back as I approached the house. I knocked loudly. I didn't want anyone being surprised. That's how people ended up dead.

Dropping my packs I pulled my gun and peeked into the windows. The place looked abandoned. Furniture, but no signs of recent activity. No food sitting on the coffee table. No movement.

Taking a deep breath I grabbed a rock from the garden and broke a window. The shattering of glass sounded like an alarm yelling to the world about an intruder. I unlatched it, crawled in then opened the front door for Haley and Jordan.

We both stood in the entranceway examining our new surroundings. A layer of dust sat on all the surfaces confirming that no one had been there for months.

Haley sighed heavily then smiled up at me. I could see it in her eyes. We were safe. She quickly made up a bed on the floor of the living room for the baby then stood up, pressing her back.

I moved our stuff inside then explored the rest of the house. Empty. A part of me had worried about discovering a body or two and wondering what I would do but luckily, we were alone. Suddenly she yelled from the kitchen. I rushed in to find her opening cabinets and smiling at me.

"It's enough for weeks," Haley said. "Maybe we should just stay here."

A new worry hit me. What would happen if we did it? I mean the place was tight, with food. Why would we move? Maybe we should just set up house here.

"What if they come back?" I asked. "And what do we do when the food runs out? It's not like the neighbors are going to help?"

Her eyes grew misty as the reality hit her. We weren't safe. Not until we got to Idaho. But I sometimes wonder if our life would have been easier if we had stayed in that nice little house in Ohio.

Chapter Fourteen

Haley

Britney cried letting me know she needed her diaper changed. I let out a long breath and went to take care of her.

"You're good at that," Tanner said. "Where did you learn?"

I snapped Britney's onesie then said, "When my mom and aunt died. I worried. I mean who would teach me? But then my friend Jenny's mom had a baby and she let me help. I even got to babysit." A sadness hit me as I wondered about that baby. Jane. Where was she? Was she all right?

While I fed Britney, Tanner made us a lunch of tuna fish salad and crackers. He'd found an unopened jar of mayonnaise, so we didn't have to worry about it being spoiled. "I saw a bar-b-q out back. I'll cook us up something hot tomorrow."

I let out a long breath as a wave of tiredness hit me. It seemed like we'd been running for half of forever. Now, finally, we were safe.

Tanner nodded to the back of the house. "There's a big king-size bed back there. You and the baby take it. I'll stay out here on the couch."

Suddenly it hit me. I was all alone with a strange boy in a strange dark house. And I wasn't freaked out about it. No, Tanner and I had moved past that nervous, belly-tumbling stage. Into the friend zone. And I'll admit, a small part of me was sort of disappointed.

But then Britney pushed her bottle away and I felt my heart melt. This little girl had become my reason for living.

We spent the next three days in that house, resting, reading, relaxing. Britney was an angel. On the third morning, I woke up to find Britney not next to me on the bed. To say I lost it would be minimizing just how freaked out I was.

I was terrified she'd rolled off the bed. Or that someone had taken her. "Tanner," I yelled as I rushed down the hall to find him asleep on the couch, Britney in the crook of his arm also asleep, an empty bottle on the table.

My heart stopped as I looked at them both of them. I swear, there is nothing cuter than a big guy with a baby. My heart melted.

Tanner must have sensed me as his eyelids fluttered then he woke to find me staring at him.

His face suddenly grew concerned, "Hey," he whispered, "I thought I'd give you a break. She's been fed and her diaper changed."

"Wow," I said, as I walked over to gently take her out of his arms. I needed to hold her. I needed to know she was alright. "Where did you learn how to do that?"

He laughed, "I've been watching you."

I smiled at him as I nuzzled her neck.

He took a deep breath then said, "I repacked everything last night, downsizing, converting your pack to the diaper bag. I moved everything else over to mine."

I nodded.

"And," he said as he pulled out a weird cloth thing from behind the couch. "I made this."

My brow furrowed in confusion as I tried to figure it out. Some kind of harness. Then I suddenly understood, a baby holder. He'd taken one of his old T-shirts, cut and tied off, and rigged a harness I could use to carry the baby.

"Oh, Tanner," I said as I handed him Britney then slipped the harness on. I poked and prodded to make sure it was strong enough then had him slip Britney into it. She woke, looking up at me, obviously upset at her nap being disturbed but then the strange sensation of hanging in mid-air hit her and she smiled, liking it.

"I can carry her and my pack," I said.

He nodded, "I've really cut yours down to just baby stuff, bottled water, and your clothes. I'll take the food, camping stuff, tent, you know, everything else.

"We can leave tomorrow," I said.

He frowned, "I was thinking today."

"No, I want to heat water and give her a bath."

Sighing, he nodded. So we spent the day getting Britney bathed, then cooked up a huge meal of canned chili, and every can we wouldn't be taking with us. He'd put the lighter stuff in his pack ready for us to leave in the morning.

After dinner, we sat on the couch watching the candle flame dance in the dark. No TV, no computers, just silence. Britney between us, sitting up, Tanner and I blocked her in so she couldn't fall over. Tanner smiled at me then reached down and let her play with his finger.

I sighed, so content. Yes, I knew the world was ending, but this moment. This was real.

We sat there in silence, a silence that began to grow awkward as I became very aware of the large boy sitting next to me. I think for the first time I was relaxed enough to think beyond the next step, the next challenge, and realized feelings inside of me were beginning to grow.

I mean, the guy was cute, strong, brave, all the things a girl instinctively is drawn to. And yes, he could be cantankerous, opinionated, and unwilling to listen to me. But, I'll be honest, I sort of liked that.

Thinking back to previous boyfriends I almost laughed. Tanner was about as opposite as you could find. I'd always been drawn to the artsy intellectual type. Tanner would never be classified as artsy.

But he wasn't a dumb hick, or shallow. Just different, just … more.

Was this sudden attraction because of our circumstances? A week into the end of the world and I was reverting to a trad wife? It hadn't been lost on me how we'd fallen into our assigned roles, me taking care of Britney. Tanner always placing himself between us and danger.

A week without electricity and I had become Jane to his Tarzan. I will be honest, deep down, I didn't mind. Things had changed. What was valuable was different. Especially if we were going to stay alive long enough to get to Idaho.

These thoughts were bouncing around in my head when I looked up to catch him staring at me with a strange look in his eyes. Almost a hungry look that made my stomach turn over and butterflies take off.

I swear, he was going to lean over and kiss me. I could feel the anticipation and joy building inside of me as I closed my eyes and leaned towards him when suddenly Jordan growled deep in his throat, ruining the moment.

The dog was faced towards the front door, the hair on his neck at full attention, his body tense, ready to attack.

"Damn," Tanner cursed as he pinched out the candle wick sending the house into darkness. He rushed to the front window and cursed again as he held his finger to his lips, telling me to be quiet.

"What?" I hissed.

"Men," he whispered back. "With guns, six or seven, on the road, they might have seen the candle."

My heart slammed in my chest. What did it mean? "Why bother us?"

"Food," he whispered without looking away from the window. Then he suddenly grabbed his pack, then mine, and pointed to the back of the house. "They're coming."

A fear filled me as I grabbed Britney off the couch and wrapped her blanket around us. Tanner held his finger to his lips again as he slowly opened the back door.

Suddenly a heavy pounding on the front door sent a cold chill down my spine. The angry voice demanded to be let in.

Tanner didn't close the door behind us, instead, putting his hand on my lower back, guiding me into the backyard and then into the trees beyond. Glass shattered behind us upping my fear.

"Just keep going," Tanner said as he wove me through the trees. We were about fifty yards in before he let out a long breath. "We can slow down."

Every instinct told me to run, as hard and as far as I could go. But I had Tanner there so things wouldn't go too terrible. Then it hit me. He hadn't stayed and fought. No, he'd done the right thing and gotten us out of there. Even now, I knew deep down he wanted to go back and tear them apart, but we were too valuable to risk.

A warmth filled me.

We spent the night working our way through the forest and then across barren farm fields. The silver moonlight covered everything in a soft glow.

"How far to the river?" I asked.

He smiled and pointed to a bridge in front of us.

"We're there?" I asked in surprise.

"Now we just need to find a boat."

"How will we buy one? I mean ..."

He frowned at me then laughed. That bad boy look in his eyes. "Who said anything about buying one?"

My stomach clenched but I held Britney and decided to let him worry about it.

When we hit the bridge, we turned off, heading west on a side road that ran along the river. We'd pass the occasional house, candlelight dancing in a window. The occasional dog would bark, warning us away. But we kept walking.

The sun was just coming up when Tanner suddenly pulled to a halt and pointed.

"A canoe?" I asked. "No way. It's not safe for Britney." My heart jumped with sudden fear. No way was I taking a baby in a canoe.

Three aluminum canoes were lined up on a beach.

"It's safer than being on the road. You know it is."

"But, why can't we find a regular boat."

He let out a long breath. "We'd have to get gas along the way. Which means getting close to people."

My heart fell. My head told me he was right, but my heart was screaming no. Tanner totally ignored me and started examining them, pulling an oar from one and putting it with another in the far boat. He dumped his pack into it then helped me out of mine and stowed it up front before holding his hand out to help me in.

"Tanner," I whined.

"I promise. This is safer. We'll take it slow. If you don't like it. We'll find something else."

Still, I hesitated, then a dog barked in the distance. A bark that was growing closer. Was someone coming? Without thinking, I let him help me in, holding Britney so tightly that she whimpered in mild discomfort.

Tanner pushed off, dipped his oar, and we slid into the middle of the river.

"Hey," Someone yelled from behind us. I looked back to see a middle-aged man with a rifle pointing towards us. Without thinking I bent over, covering Britney, praying I wasn't about to be shot.

Tanner became a windmill with the oar, pushing us farther and farther away. All I could do was hold my breath, waiting for that fatal shot. Praying, and cursing. All while the boat rocked side to side, scaring me. But the man never fired. I don't know if he determined a canoe wasn't worth killing someone over or what. But we lived.

Twenty minutes later I felt Tanner slow down and turned to see him smiling like a little boy who'd gotten away with sneaking his mom's cookies.

Once again, my heart melted, and I realized I was in love with Tanner Parks.

Chapter Fifteen

Tanner

Who knew canoes were so easy? I mean, once you got a rhythm going. Kept things balanced. It was a breeze.

New fact. The Ohio River had been turned into a bunch of lakes. It had so many locks and dams that there was almost no current. A little, but not like the Hudson. I'd paddle down the middle, reach a lock then beach the canoe, hump our gear to the other side of the lock. Jordan and Haley would hang out while I ran back and dragged the canoe then we were off again.

We fell into a pattern. Twelve hours of rowing with a break for lunch that we'd eat in the middle of the river, then I'd find a quiet place to camp for the night. I know, too easy. We'd pass people fishing on the shore. Some would wave, others would scowl. I ignored them but made a mental note to add a fishing pole to our stuff.

I'd never been fishing, but how hard could it be? I mean, I was rowing a canoe, something I never anticipated.

We made about thirty or forty miles a day as we passed through farms then subdivisions intermixed with small towns. I made a point of going through Cincinnati at night and found a place three or four miles after the last building.

On the fourth night, I looked over at Haley sleeping, the baby in her arms inside her sleeping bag. I'll be honest, my heart sort of melted. I mean she was such a good mom. Oh yeah, and beautiful. Smart, kind, all the things a guy likes.

No bitching or complaining all the time. No demanding I fix things I couldn't fix. Just your basically perfect girl.

Back off, I told myself. Haley wasn't interested that way. To her, I was bodyguard, free labor, and pet monster.

Her eyes fluttered open to find me staring at her. She gave me a quick smile then checked the baby to make sure everything was okay.

"We need to get food, diapers. We're okay on formula but if we find more that'd be good."

She nodded. "How? Where?"

I shrugged, "The next town, I'll go in and see what I can find."

Her eyes grew big, "We'll go together."

I wondered if it was because she didn't want to be left alone or hated the idea of missing out.

When we approached a small city, I wondered where we were at. I mean, they don't put signs on the river announcing you'd just entered Podunk Ohio. My gut told me this was going to be a problem.

I beached the canoe then helped Haley out, Jordan immediately began sniffing, searching for that special place to do his business.

"Come on," I said as I touched Haley's lower back. She shuddered and gave me a strange look. I immediately pulled back, pretending like I hadn't touched her when I shouldn't have. Shaking my head, I tried to focus on where we were going, but in the back of my mind, I was working over this new reality. Back home, before the world ended, girls hadn't been a real problem. I mean, a big guy, a fighter, sort of good-looking. No, they hadn't been a problem. But then they hadn't been girls like Haley. I was beginning to realize there were no other girls like Haley.

We passed through a small park and into a subdivision of nice homes. Haley glanced over at me, silently asking what we should do next.

I took a deep breath and tried to figure it out.

"Come on," I said as I pointed to the road that ran along the bank of the river. It only took us a few blocks to find the part of town that supported all these homes. Typical main street with strip malls and a large supermarket.

I smiled at Haley then led her to the grocery store. I didn't know what I'd used to pay for stuff, but this was our best bet. Unfortunately, the place was darker than a closet. I put my hands against the glass door and peered inside.

"It's empty," a voice growled behind me.

I spun around to find an old, grizzled man. He spit tobacco juice then shook his head. "Ain't nothing left. Two weeks and she's cleaned out. Nothing coming in."

My heart fell.

The old man glanced at our packs then the baby and almost smiled before his eyes grew very sad. "It's going to get rough. People are already freaking out." He then looked at Jordan and shook his head. "You ever hear about them ancient sieges. People all stuck in a castle. Things are fine, the walls keep the bad guys out. But then the food starts running out. It never ends pretty. They eat the rats first, then the cats, and finally the dogs. Maybe each other.

Haley stared at me with wide eyes. We'd talked about it, at least around the edges. I mean that was why we were headed to Idaho. But I think this was the first time when it began to sink in.

"Don't believe me?" he said as he pointed up the street.

My gut tightened as a group of about a dozen men armed with clubs and knives were walking down the street towards us.

"I'm out of here," the man said, giving the approaching group another look. He turned and walked away.

My gut tightened as I tried to figure out what to do. We needed food. But I also needed to protect what little we had left. And there was Haley and the baby. These guys didn't look like a welcoming committee of housewives.

"You coming?" the man said over his shoulder, obviously inviting us to join him. I could see it all laid out. He wanted us away from this group.

I nudged Haley to follow the man while looking over my shoulder. They were about a hundred yards away. Would they chase us? What was the fastest way back to the canoe? See I knew going ashore was stupid. But we didn't have a choice.

The old man ducked around the corner of the building then stuck his head back around the edge and motioned for us to hurry. Haley and I scurried after him. We followed him for two blocks. Down a shadowy alley, across a street, behind some homes, and then down another alley.

Suddenly he stopped, looked around to make sure no one was watching, and pushed a board aside, holding it while motioning us in.

I took a breath, were we walking into a serial killer's secret lair? That'd just be my luck. A match flared and the darkness washed away to reveal a small room with a couch, an ancient box-type TV with those long antenna things. Now useless without electricity. Plus, the place smelled moldy. Like wet plywood.

Wow, had this guy been here since the fifties?

"Grab a seat," he said as he reached over to ruffle Jordan's fur. "Hang out for a bit and they'll disappear. You lot can get away without any problems."

My stomach tightened. I'd left our canoe. What if someone took it? And we still needed food.

The man lit one of those T-lite candles and set a pot of water over it.

"Tea is about all I can offer."

Haley unwrapped the baby and laid her on the couch. She looked up at him and asked, "We need diapers."

He laughed and shook his head, "You lot are going to have to figure how to do without. People lived a long time before disposable diapers."

My heart fell when I saw the fear in Haley's eyes. Yes, people had lived without the benefits of modern civilization, but they knew what they were doing. Not starting out from scratch.

I dropped my pack and rolled my shoulders to work out some of the pain when I heard

Haley gasp. Turning around our new friend was standing there with a pistol pointed at my gut.

"Sorry," he said with a shrug, "But like I said, all I've got is tea. You guys probably have food."

My heart fell. I had been such an idiot, walking into his trap. I'd even delivered our stuff directly to his home.

Without thinking, my hand started to drift to the gun in my belt.

"Tanner," Haley snapped, stopping me.

The old man laughed, "You're wife is smart. I ain't got anything to lose."

A shameful guilt filled me. How had I allowed this to happen? God, I was such an idiotic fool.

"Very careful," he said, his pistol never wavering. "Put your guns on the floor and kick them over here. Both of them."

My gut fell. I should have hidden my second gun. Lesson learned, I said to myself. If I lived through the next few minutes, I'd make sure not to screw up this bad again.

I used two fingers and slowly placed my guns on the floor and then gently nudged them to him.

"On the couch, next to your wife."

Swallowing hard, I scrambled to figure a way out of this mess. Once I was down on the couch, I couldn't act fast. But a wrong move and this guy was going to start firing. I remembered the baby's mom getting killed the last time I charged in like a bull.

"Tanner," Haley said as she took my hand and pulled me towards the couch.

I hesitated, shooting him an ugly look, letting him know what I'd do to him if I could get my hands around his neck.

The old guy actually cringed, obviously embarrassed at himself. "Like I said, things have gotten bad. There isn't even garbage to pick through. Ain't anyone wasting food anymore. And believe me, no one is sharing."

"So stealing is the answer?" Haley said. "If you had asked, we would have shared."

Jordan growled deep in his throat. I grabbed his collar, I didn't need him going off. I mean, it would take a lot to get him upset, but ever since we got the baby his protective juices seemed to be on full alert.

The guy's cheeks grew red as he pointed his gun at my pack and said, "Let's see what you've got."

I had to sit there while he rummaged through our stuff pulling out the food. A bag of rice, a box of Pop-Tarts, beef jerky, and all the baby formula.

"Every calory helps," he said as he set the formula aside.

"No," Haley gasped.

He shrugged but made sure his pistol covered me. "You can find more."

My heart hurt at the thought of the baby going without. No, this was not going to stand. I clenched my teeth, forcing myself to not erupt. Haley and the baby were too close. Too vulnerable.

"I'm sorry," he said as he stepped back from the bags stuffing my pistols in his belt. "You can go."

I froze. Was this a trick? Were we going to get shot in the back? It didn't really matter, I realized. Without that food, we'd never make it.

"Please," Haley begged.

The baby, sensing her distress, began to cry. Unusual for her. But I knew I needed to get them out of there. "Let's go," I said with a heavy sigh.

Haley glanced at me, obviously surprised that I was being so meek, accepting this. What had happened to her pet monster?

"Go," I said as I stood and grabbed my pack then hers.

She hesitated, unable to accept what was happening. "Please," she begged. "Leave us one can of formula."

The guy shook his head then nodded to the door.

I somehow got Haley and the baby outside. Just get them away, I kept telling myself. The wood door closed behind me and I could hear him doing something inside to lock it.

Haley continued to hesitate, obviously not wanting to leave. "Tanner?" she whispered.

"Shush," I said as I took her arm and gently pulled her to the corner.

"We can't ..."

"Come on Haley, do you really think I'm letting him get away with this crap?"

She paused, staring up at me.

"Stay here. I'll be right back," I said as I dropped the packs around the corner.

"What? No!"

Ignoring her, I hurried back down the alley. I needed to do this my way. Fast and furious. I didn't really think things through and let my bull loose in the China shop. Lowering my shoulder I slammed through the wooden door like I was pushing through a shower curtain.

The old man was on the couch, a pop tart in his mouth, the pistols on the table in front of him. The look of shock in his eyes was priceless. I could tell he'd never expected me to come back.

His hand reached for the pistol, mine reached for his neck. I won.

Grabbing the hand holding the pistol I kept it pointed away from me as I lifted him up off the couch, dangling his feet a foot off the ground as my fingers clamped down. I knew if he got his hand free, he'd shoot me deader than dead. So I clamped down even harder.

His face turned blue as his eyes bugged out.

I held him there in mid-air until his feet stopped kicking and his head slumped in death. Letting him drop I took a deep breath as I tried to slow my racing heart. I had killed again. It was easier this time.

Somewhere deep in my soul, I feared I was going to find it got easier each time.

Chapter Sixteen

Haley

The silence was killing me. Tanner dipped his oar, pushing us along, pretending like nothing had happened. But I knew it was eating him up inside.

Twisting, I looked over my shoulder to find him glowering at the world. Either he was pissed off at being trapped, fooled. Or upset at killing that man. I know he killed him. He wouldn't have been able to walk out of there with all our food and an extra pistol.

My heart broke seeing the pain in his eyes, but Britney started to fuss. She didn't like being laid down on her blankets in the bottom of the boat. She preferred to be up, seeing where we were going.

Sighing, I wallowed in my melting heart and just thanked God that she hadn't been hurt. We had escaped with our lives. But we still needed supplies. Idaho was so far away.

We spent the rest of the day working our way down the river. My soul hurt thinking about how things had changed. The towns were quiet, the countryside even quieter. Twice we passed towns on fire, people scrambling to get away with their last food.

Tanner just kept paddling. He'd been right about the boat. It was so much safer than being stuck on land. A shiver shot down my spine when I thought about what we might be facing.

That night, in the tent, I lay with Britney in my arms and stared into the dark wondering about what was going to happen to us. We had to find food. Suddenly, Tanner cried out in his sleep, twisting, and turning.

"Tanner," I whispered trying to wake him from his nightmare.

His hand shot up into the air, his fingers clamped like he was trying to squeeze the life out of something. My heart broke as I reached over to touch his shoulder. "Tanner, you're dreaming. Wake up."

His eyes shot open, filled with a look of shame that surprised me. I mean the boy was always so together. To see him like this just seemed wrong. It was as if the rock in the middle of a raging river suddenly cracked in two, threatening to let go and crumble into a thousand pieces.

As I watched he slowly pulled himself together, taking deep breaths as he centered himself. Finally, he shot me a weak smile. "I'm okay."

My heart went out to him. He was living through terror and his first thought was to reassure me.

Settling back down I watched as he closed his eyes and slowly drifted off to sleep. My mind wandered to just how much I had come to rely upon him. Not just for his physical strength. The guy was stronger than a horse. I could barely lift his pack up off the ground and he threw it around like a bookbag.

And not just for his bravery. Although, that was the difference between me and Britney being alive and not being alive.

No, I relied upon him for more. So much more. The thought of losing him sent a bolt of pure panic shooting through me.

He carried so many burdens. Things that would be easy to take for granted. His need to step between me and any danger. His permanent vigilance. Constantly evaluating threats, seeking alternatives.

A tear formed at the corner of my eye as I realized there was nothing, I could do to ease his burdens. Not really.

Britney woke me that morning with her wet diaper whimper. I glanced over and saw that Tanner was gone. My heart jumped until I heard him outside breaking wood for a fire.

Closing my eyes, I allowed myself to be grateful for him. To put aside the thousands of problems we faced and just be thankful for a minute. Then I crawled out of the sleeping bag and began the next day.

For the next few days, we kept to the side of the river as it broadened. The current was stronger with a weak wind out of the east. We had almost reached the Mississippi when

Tanner shifted his paddling and brought us into a small marina. I frowned back at him, silently asking why.

He let out a long breath. "I can't paddle upstream all the way to Montana. It will take too long."

"Okay," I said hesitantly.

Nodding, he pointed out an aluminum boat with an old outboard engine. Rigid this time, Aluminum, not a rubber zodiac. The kind of boat good-ole-boys took out fishing.

Parking us next to the boat, he helped me over into it and then started storing our gear. We were almost done when someone suddenly yelled, "Hey," followed by the unmistakable click of a shotgun shell being pumped into a chamber.

Tanner froze then slowly stepped off onto the wooden dock, once again putting himself between me and a young guy approaching us, his brow furrowed in confusion.

My heart raced. Was Tanner going to force this guy to give up his boat? See, that was where my mind was at when it came to Tanner. It never occurred to me that we weren't going to end up with the boat.

"You can't steal that," the man said as he made sure the shotgun was pointed directly at Tanner's gut.

Tanner moved his hands away from the pistol in his belt. "We'll buy it."

The guy, maybe mid-20s, with long hair tied back with a rubber band, scoffed. "Money's no good anyway."

Tanner shrugged. "This boat isn't doing you much good, tied off to a pier."

"Don't matter. You can't have it."

There was a long awkward silence. I held my breath, terrified Tanner was going to do something.

"We can find a different boat," I said hoping to give him an out.

Tanner ignored me then said, "We'll trade a pistol for the boat, and a handful of bullets."

Of course, I thought. We had three of them now. Yes, this was the perfect answer.

The guy frowned then slowly smiled. "Yes, that will work. Like you said, the boat isn't doing me any good anyway."

"And gas," Tanner added. "It's a .38 snubbed nose revolve, like new. And a couple of life jackets."

The guy's eyes grew then he nodded. "Sure. You'll have to siphon it from the tank."

I sighed, nobody was going to get killed today.

"And food."

The guy scowled and shook his head. "No deal."

Tanner sighed. twenty minutes later we were buzzing down the river making the turn north onto the mighty Mississippi river. The Big Muddy, they called it, and I could see why. The river was brown and big. Real big.

I felt a tremor of trepidation as the boat picked up speed. Visions of Huck Finn filled my head as I looked at the farmland lining the banks. We were going to have to go ashore and find food. A nervousness filled me. Every time we went into a town something bad happened. But we didn't have a choice. Besides, now we were going to have to get gas.

Tanner guided us over to the side then twisted away from a large log drifting down the river. I looked back, the wind ruffled his hair, the sun beat down on his face and the boy was smiling for the first time in days.

His strong jaw needed a shave, his scruffy beard had a red tint that made me think of ancient Vikings. My heart melted at the joy in his eyes.

We were about five miles south of St. Louis when we came upon a huge barge and tugboat grounded on a sand bar. Just like every truck and car, the EMP had disabled the boat. I wondered how long it had drifted down the river until it cam to rest on a sand bar, fifty yards from the beach.

Tanner pushed the engine aside to steer us around the huge barges when a man came out on the deck of the tugboat and started waving his hands, shouting at us.

My breath caught in my throat. All I could see was another threat. Avoid people, I thought as I glanced back at Tanner.

His brow was furrowed in determination as he pushed us farther out. Then suddenly he let out a long breath and throttled back on the engine. We slowed until he could keep us centered in the river. Just enough to stop from drifting back.

The man stopped waving and yelled, "Can you take me ashore?"

Tanner sighed then slowly turned towards the tugboat.

"Tanner," I gasped, unwilling to take a risk.

"Maybe he has food," he answered as he drew close then stopped about ten feet away.

The man watched us then yelled. "Can't swim, crew left me the second day. Can I get a lift ashore?"

Tanner hesitated, "Do you have any food?"

The man smiled, "We were taking pig iron to New Orleans. That's a two-week trip."

"And that means?" Tanner asked still holding the boat in the middle of the river.

The man smiled, "That means I got enough for three people for two weeks. Or did have before half of it spoiled."

Tanner shot me a quick smile then pointed the boat towards the tugboat. The man stepped off the tug onto our small aluminum boat like a man born to the river. He gave me a quick smile then tipped his hat.

Jordan sniffed him, withholding judgment.

When we pulled into the bank the man nimbly jumped ashore without getting wet. Then turned back to us with a frown. "Do you guys know what is going on? I ain't heard a thing, the boat died, saw a dozen other boats drift by, deader than my great-grandpa.

Tanner told him what we knew. The man's face slowly turned white then he took a deep breath. "That was what I was afraid of."

"Where you headed?" Tanner asked.

The man pointed south, "Wife's parents have a farm, she and the kids will head there. I'll be there in two days or so."

"We'll good luck," Tanner said as he dropped the boat into reverse and pulled away from the bank. Within minutes he had us tied off next to the tugboat and took Britney so I could climb up.

"Do you really think they have food?"

Tanner shrugged then pulled his pistol and led the way into the cabin. We had to leave the door open to get enough light. Suddenly, Tanner yelled then held up a large bag of flour followed by a box of powdered milk.

Such simple things, I thought as I let out a long breath, we weren't going to starve. At least not this week.

Chapter Seventeen

Tanner

That tugboat was a treasure trove. I mean it had everything. Food, a fishing pole and tackle, a canvas bag full of tools, but best of all, a five-gallon gas can. Now I could fill two of them and have enough, so I didn't have to stop at noon.

We spent the night aboard, sleeping in bunks, and then hit the river the next morning. We turned west onto the Missouri just north of St Louis. I kept us centered in the new river and wondered how much further. A thousand miles?

The boat was loaded, between the four of us, and our supplies, it was low in the water. About halfway past the big city, the morning air was shattered with gunfire. Haley instinctively cringed as she bent over Britney, protecting her.

I swung away from the sound. It wasn't a single shot, more like a firefight with a dozen guns firing, each reaching out to try and kill someone.

Gritting my teeth, I sent up a silent thank you that we didn't have to work our way through that. Things were getting bad. Two weeks worth of food. That was what most cities had. Even out here in the mid-west, cities were going to be hurting.

Of course, just when you thought things couldn't go bad, they did, the engine suddenly started coughing and sputtering. Haley's eyes grew to the size of dinner plates as she looked at the engine, then the shoreline, then at me, silently begging me to fix things.

Cursing under my breath I feathered the engine trying to make it last long enough to get us to the beach. I didn't want to drift down the river and end up in New Orleans.

The engine continued to sputter. I checked the gas can, more than enough, I swear it was like it just wasn't getting enough fuel.

"Tanner?" Haley whispered.

I ignored her and focused on keeping things running long enough. Finally, I spotted a boat tied off to a dock. Using the last of the engine I got us in next to the dock and thew a line around a cleat.

Only when we were secure was I able to let out a long breath.

"What happened?" Haley asked.

All I could do was shrug then look around to make sure we weren't going to be attacked immediately. Grabbing a blanket I threw it over our supplies to hide them from prying eyes. Haley saw it and immediately pulled a corner to hide the food.

"Stay there," I said as I began taking the engine off the back and laying it on the dock. Suddenly a dozen shots rang out, just blocks away. My gut dropped as I scrambled to get the engine apart.

"What do you think it is?" Haley asked from the front of the boat. I ignored her as I pulled the fuel filter and blew through it hoping to clear it out.

Again shots rang out, closer this time. Like a running battle that was about to spill over us.

Gritting my teeth, I tried to force my fingers not to shake as I fumbled to get the filter back in line and the fuel hose hooked up.

"Tanner," Haley called. I turned to see her pointing. Three men were kneeling behind a car, rifles pointed up the street.

Swallowing hard, I finished getting things hooked up, pumped the bulb, and pulled the cord. The engine coughed then died. I swore under my breath as I repeated the process. This time the engine caught and held.

Sighing internally, I slipped the line off the cleat and headed out into the middle of the river just as the three men opened up firing down the street. Thankfully, away from us.

Haley shielded Britney as I worked us up the river, desperate to just get away. It seemed like the city went on forever. Twice I saw fires that I was pretty sure no one would ever put out. There were more shots and a blood-curdling scream that still eats at my soul.

But we made it through the suburbs and broke into open country. That flat midwestern country of corn fields, prairie grass, and big sky. Haley looked back and gave me a sad smile. "We need to stop. Get set up for the night."

I nodded, she was right, I wanted to put distance between us and that hell back in St Louis, but she was right. I started scanning the bank to find an empty place we could pull in. Somewhere away from roads, farmhouses, the kind of place with distance, separation.

Luckily, I found a small cut with trees and a steep bank. The kind of place where I could hide a fire. I beached the boat and helped Haley out. She shot me a quick smile, obviously approving of my selection. But Britney started fussing, pulling her attention. While she dealt with the baby, I quickly set up the tent then gathered firewood.

After dinner, Haley and I sat with out backs to a log and stared into the fire. Britney was in the tent, Jordan next to my leg his head on his paws.

"It is so far," Haley said with a sad sigh.

All I could do was nod. "One step at a time."

A silence fell over us and an awkward tingle traveled through my body as I realized I was sitting next to a beautiful girl, A fire dancing in the dark. I mean, could anything be more romantic? And I am pretty sure Haley was very aware of the situation. The tenseness in her

185

body, the quick looks she shot me. I swear, it was like we were in middle school and had just discovered the other sex.

Every instinct in me demanded I kiss her. Of course that fought with the fear of ruining everything. I swear I was getting to the point where I didn't care and was willing to risk it when Briteny suddenly began to whimper in the tent.

Haley looked up at me and I saw a mix of regret and thankfulness in her eyes. As if she was too terrified of what might happen between us.

Taking a deep breath, I shifted to let her get up and see to the baby. But I couldn't stop from cursing under my breath. Haley heard me and shot me a sad smile. I didn't know if it was because she was feeling the same frustration or because she felt sorry for the stupid boy thinking things he shouldn't.

For the next five days, we worked our way up the Missouri river. We would pass abandoned tugboats and barges. Twice we saw families down close to the river in tents. I wondered if they'd been kicked out of their homes. Or lost between places when the asteroid hit.

It took almost a full day to drag our stuff and the boat around one of the dams. But we were able to use the locks on the second damn.

I was able to find cars for gas, or one time, a tractor in the middle of a field. Everything had just stopped where it was when it all went down. I'd gas up then go further upriver. I didn't want to hang out where I'd just stolen some gas.

But I'd always find a lonely place. After getting the camp set up, I'd hit the river with my new fishing pole. Anything to make our food last a little longer. Haley was amazing with the things she knew. Like who knew wild onions grew next to rivers? Or that the best bait was grasshoppers.

"Two cousins, a brother, and an uncle who liked to camp," she said with a smile.

My heart broke thinking about all she had lost. Of course, I thought about my brother Johnny. Had he made shore? Would he ever see the note I left him? It didn't matter. I would never know. We were cut off and would never talk to each other again.

One asteroid had knocked us back a hundred years. Maybe more. What would happen?

As if reading my mind, Haley said, "We need to get to Idaho. We'll be safe on my grandfather's farm."

I was tempted to push back. We had no idea who or what would be waiting for us when we got there. If we got there. But I bit my tongue. It didn't do any good busting her bubble.

That became our world, the river. We bypassed all the drama on the shore. We made at least fifty miles a day. And hey, it was sort of great just sharing a boat with Haley and the baby.

Of course, things never last. We were in the middle of the river when I hit something. I swear I didn't see anything, but the engine jerked out of my hand as it slammed to a halt. The boat lurched almost throwing me off my seat.

Haley squealed as she twisted to protect the baby.

How? Why? I mean the river was a chocolate brown full of mud from the Rockies and I couldn't see two inches under the top.

I immediately started scrambling as the boat began to drift back down the river, the current pulling at us. I lifted the engine and winced. It looked like the propeller had been chewed up and spit out. One blade was missing, the other two were twisted pretzels.

Haley's eyes grew big.

All I could do was shrug then look back down river and wonder where we would come ashore.

My guts began to worry, I mean we could go all the way to the last dam. And if we got caught in the overflow there was nothing stopping us from being pushed over the top.

"Well, this sucks," I said as I started pulling off my boots, then my shirt.

"What ..." Haley started to ask.

I ignored her as I shucked my jeans and slipped over the side of the boat. Coming up, I shook the water from my hair then smiled at Haley to reassure her. "Hand me that rope. I'll tow us ashore."

"Tanner," she gasped.

I started to use one arm and my legs to pull the boat when I bumped against something. My heart jumped until I realized it was the bottom. Shaking my head I realized the river was only three feet deep at this point.

Shaking my head I stood up and laughed at Haley's shocked face. She stared at me for a long minute then suddenly she blushed and looked away.

I mean what was the big deal, I had boxers on. Shrugging, I started for the beach. When I had her and the baby safely ashore, I sighed heavily and said. "We might have to start walking sooner than we wanted to. That lower section is torn up. We either find a new engine, or we walk."

Haley frowned as she looked up the river. "We've still got three states. I say we try to find a new engine or boat." She turned back to me then quickly away before saying. "Get dressed."

I laughed, it seemed Miss Haley Conrad thought I was hot. There are worse things in life. Like having a broke engine, but for some reason, I couldn't stop smiling.

Chapter Eighteen

Haley

Boys should not look that good. It gave them too much power. When Tanner had undressed, I had been unable to look away, then he jumped in the water to tow us ashore. Typical hero stuff, and stands up, water dripping off his hard chest. The wounds on his left forearm and right shoulder reminded me of his heroics. I swear it was like a Viking god rising up out of the ocean.

Our boat engine was all messed up and all I could do was not look at him. My face would flame as thoughts flashed through my mind.

"Get dressed," I told him as I focused on Britney.

He laughed behind me, but he did what I asked.

"This place looks good. Let's get set up," he said as he started unloading the boat.

A sand bar with a six-foot bank, driftwood, and cottonwood trees along the bank. Farm fields beyond, full of corn stubble. They hadn't put in the spring crop before the EMP hit. A road about a half mile from the river and a few farmhouses.

"I'm sorry," Tanner said as he put the tent together. "I should have seen it. The snag."

I laughed, "Tanner, the water is thicker than a chocolate milk shake. I'm amazed we've made it this far."

He laughed then looked at the setting sun in the west. "I'll go look for a replacement tomorrow. There are a bunch of farms near a river. They should have boats, engines."

"Shouldn't we all go?" I asked as my stomach clenched. The thought of being left alone terrified me. What if something happened to him?

He sighed then shook his head. "It will be better if I go alone. I can go farther, faster, and let's be honest. No one is going to want to mess with me. Not unless I have a pretty girl along."

My heart fell, he was right, which just made it even worse.

We settled in for the night, I fed Britney while he cooked up a can of stew we'd gotten from the tugboat. After we'd cleaned up, we settled down and let Britney play between us. She was rolling over and I was pretty sure she was going to start crawling any day. She was already pushing herself up on her knees.

"She's so amazing," Tanner said as he shook his head. My heart melted seeing the love in his eyes. He'd die for this little girl. There was no doubt in my mind. That thought was followed by the awareness that he was once again placing himself in danger for us.

"You will be careful," I whispered in half prayer.

He laughed and said, "When have I ever not been careful?"

Now it was my time to laugh as I slapped at his shoulder. Suddenly, that oh-so-familiar awkwardness settled over us. God, I swear it was always there. A heavy weight holding us down. Reminding me what I couldn't have.

Tanner sighed heavily then said, "I need to get some sleep. I'll be off before sunrise. I'll leave one of the pistols with you."

All I could do was nod as my heart broke a little more.

The next morning, good to his word, he handed me a pistol then shocked me by leaning down and kissing the top of my head. "I'll try to be back before nightfall. Even if I don't find what we need."

All I could do was clench my teeth to stop from begging him not to go. A deep dread filled me. I would never see him again. And I hadn't told him all I needed to.

He kissed Britney's cheek making her giggle and turned and left us. Once more stepping into danger.

Jordan trotted after him, but Tanner held up his hand and said, "Stay with them." Then turned and disappeared into the morning gray.

"Oh, Britney," I whispered as I held her close. "I love him."

The baby gurgled then pulled at my hair. I could only stare in the direction Tanner had gone. Please be careful, I prayed. Please don't do something stupid. Come back to me. Yes, I was aware it was an unrequited love, the worst kind of love. But a girl can't help feeling what she feels.

I mean the boy was big, strong, brave, and sweet. He could change a diaper if he had to, but he could fight off a pack of monsters if he had to. What girl wouldn't fall in love?

Closing my eyes, I thought about the way he smelled. We had a bar of Irish Spring soap, and he used it every night. My insides melted thinking about him.

Sighing to myself, I decided to focus on chores. I spent the morning boiling water and washing diapers. After lunch, I put Britney down after her bottle then climbed the bank to look for Tanner. The sun was like a hammer hitting me with waves of heat. The air was stiller than a scared rabbit.

No Tanner of course. No, things wouldn't be that simple. Jordan nosed my hand, silently asking for a pet, he didn't like being left behind. His man was off having adventures without him.

"He'll be back in a bit," I assured the dog, but my stomach refused to believe it. Sighing, I looked for something to do and came up empty.

Everything seemed so unimportant without Tanner there.

"Come on," I said to Jordan as I tapped my leg before sliding down the bank to our camp. "Let's grab a nap. Maybe he'll be back before we wake up."

The dog wagged his tail, obviously liking the idea. We crawled into the tent, I opened the vents to get a cross breeze before laying down next to Britney, Jordan took the other side.

Sleep came quickly as I thought about Tanner and the way he looked wading ashore. I swear it was in one of the most perfect dreams when something pulled me back to reality. Jordan growled low in his throat.

My heart jumped as I heard a noise out in our camp.

"Tanner?" I called as I rushed to unzip the tent and get outside. "NO!" I gasped. A strange man stood in the middle of our camp holding my pistol.

I'd left it on top of my pack. I didn't like having it in the tent with Britney.

Jordan growled then barked. I instinctively grabbed his collar before he could get himself shot. My insides fluttered with worry as I looked at the stranger. Maybe mid-forties, tall but thin. A John Deere ball cap and two weeks of beard.

Everything said local farmer, but his eyes made me cringe and want to run. Cold, dead eyes. Like a shark's. The man looked through me like I didn't have a soul or anything of worth.

"You alone?" he asked, his brow furrowing as he looked around.

It was at that moment that Britney decided to cry out from in the tent, letting me know she wouldn't mind being changed. A small cry then silence. She'd give me ten minutes then cry again just in case I was too stupid to understand what she wanted the first time.

The man's cold eyes darted to the tent and the baby's sound.

I froze for a second then said, "My husband should be back soon." A multidimensional lie. He wasn't my husband. Never would be. And he might never be coming back. But this jerk didn't need to know that.

The man scoffed then shook his head. "He left you here? Alone?"

Biting my tongue I forced myself not to reply. The last thing I needed to do was get into an argument with this idiot. And yes, every instinct inside of me demanded that I defend Tanner. But Britney was a higher priority at the moment, staying alive for her was pretty high on my list of duties.

Jordan pulled at the hand holding his collar. The man instantly shifted his aim towards the dog. "You better keep him quiet. Although, I guess I'll have to kill him anyway. He'd just get in the way."

"What, No," I gasped as I pushed Jordan back to stand between him and the man.

He raised an eyebrow and shook his head. "You know how this goes. Cooperate and I'll let you and the baby live."

My stomach fell. It wasn't just his words, but the matter-of-fact coldness in his tone. It was as if he was telling me he was going to charge me five bucks for a cup of coffee.

"Tanner will kill you," I said. The words just came out. And I knew deep in my soul that they were true. I would be used and cast aside. But Tanner would exact a terrible revenge.

The man waved his gun, telling me to step aside so he could kill our dog then take me.

"No," I said with my fiercest determination.

The man raised an eyebrow, "You got a baby to worry about. If I start shooting, there is no telling where the bullets might go."

My world crumbled as I realized I would do what ever this man wanted to save Britney.

"Please," I begged. "I'll tie him up."

The man was actually thinking it through. Could he take me if the dog was tied up? Would it be faster? These and a thousand other thoughts were running through his mind when a sudden shape flew off the top of the bank onto my attacker.

A large, very masculine entity in the shape of one Tanner Parks. The man never stood a chance, Tanner hit him with a flying tackle that carried them both into the river.

I gasped as I watched Tanner come up first, his hand around the man's neck. A thrill filled me, to be rescued and I'll be honest, a small part of me wanted the man to suffer. He had threatened me and mine. He should be punished.

But I remembered Tanner's nightmares. "No," I said as I pulled at his shoulder. "Don't kill him."

Tanner had the man pinned under the water, his face being driven into the mud while his knee held down the arm with the pistol. Tanner tugged the gun out of the man's fist before leaning back and pulling him up out of the water.

Shooting me a frustrated look, Tanner shook his head then said to the man. "You live a little longer because she wants it. Please, give me a reason to ignore her and I'll kill you deader than dead."

A calmness filled me, Tanner would not have to live with another tragedy, and I wouldn't be filled with guilt. But most of all, I knew that with Tanner in my life, I need never fear.

"Get loaded," Tanner said as he dragged the man up out of the water and tied him to a tree. "I got an engine, we need to be going."

"Why?" I asked.

Tanner laughed, "Because they might want it back when they find it missing."

Rolling my eyes, I could only sigh as I hurried to get Britney changed then the boat packed. I swear within fifteen minutes we were on the river headed west. Tanner looked over his shoulder at the man still tied to the tree.

It reminded me of the man we'd left on the banks of the Hudson tied to his chair. Well, it was better than killing him.

Once we were a few miles further up the river I was able to relax. But it was two days before I could shake the cringy memory of that man's eyes crawling over me like I was a piece of meat.

But I woke the third day past it. A person can't dwell on all the bad things in the world. There just isn't enough time. Looking back I caught Tanner staring off into the distance. I could read his mind. He was looking for danger, looking for hidden snags or terror from the beaches always protecting us.

It was only then that I felt my heart shift. I was in love with Tanner and there was nothing I could do about it.

A sadness washed over me as I thought about before. In the olden days, two weeks earlier. If I'd liked a boy I'd have flirted, maybe gotten a friend to let him know how I felt. You know the tried-and-true methods. But those had been mere boys. Not men like Tanner.

God, I wished my Mom was here to tell me what to do. I looked back at him, the setting sun highlighting his sharp cheekbones and strong stubbled jaw and felt my world shift from beneath me. No, I couldn't just live like this. Live in a self-induced purgatory.

Slowly a plan began to form.

That afternoon when we stopped, I told Tanner that he was in charge of the baby. I was going to take a bath. I grabbed a towel, and the bar of soap and headed to the end of the sandbar to the other side of a tree that had fallen into the river, creating a small, still pool.

I peeked over the edge to make sure Tanner was where I left him and quickly disrobed and got into the river. After a thorough wash, I got out, dried off, then got dressed in my new outfit. Daisy Duke cutoffs and one of Tanner's flannel shirts tied off, exposing a lot of skin.

If this didn't get him interested, then nothing ever would.

Holding my breath, I stepped over the tree and started for the camp. Please, I silently begged. Please see me. The real me.

Biting my back teeth, I made sure to sway my hips a little more than necessary. I needn't have bothered, Tanner had his head down talking to Britney.

Stopping, I forced myself to not scowl.

Tanner looked up, his jaw didn't drop. He didn't become all bugged-eyed. Instead, he shook his head and looked down at Britney.

My heart sank. I had failed. The cruelest of rejections.

"You can't dress like that," he said without looking up.

"Why?" I demanded as I put my hands on my hips. I wanted to clobber the idiot and he was telling me what to do!

Taking a deep breath he let it out slowly. "Because it isn't fair. You can't dress like that and expect me to keep my hands off you."

My heart threatened to soar.

"I mean," he continued. "It is hard enough on a normal day not to pull you into my arms and kiss you for the next three weeks. It's not fair."

"I wouldn't push you away," I whispered, unable to believe the words coming out of my mouth.

Chapter Nineteen

Tanner

My body screamed at me. Demanded I take what it wanted. The girl was heart-stopping beautiful. Enticing, with a touch of innocence that called to my soul. And she was hinting that she might sort of feel the same way about me. Maybe. Possibly.

Thankfully, I was smart enough to exercise some control.

Everything disappeared as I looked into her eyes. The girl was nervous, worried. Why? Then it hit me. The outfit, that wiggle in her walk, the look in her eyes. This was a girl interested.

I'm not an idiot. I knew that look, but everything told me to be careful. This was Haley we were talking about. Her heart was too precious.

"Um …" I started. "You do realize how gorgeous you are. Right?"

"Do you think so?"

I swear, she did coy very well.

I laughed, then remembered I was holding Britney. Without really thinking it through I put the baby back into the tent then turned to Haley as I held her shoulders and looked deep into her eyes again. "Just so you know, I am going to kiss you."

She smiled just a bit then looked up at my lips. "Why are you waiting?"

That was all I needed, we came together like an unstoppable force. Nothing could have kept us apart.

It was as if the world disappeared, there was only Haley. For half of forever, we kissed and touched, driving each other higher and higher until I pulled back suddenly.

Haley frowned with confusion as she tried to focus.

"We can't," I said. Probably the hardest words to ever come out of my mouth. I was already kicking myself.

"What? Why?" she asked as her brow furrowed.

I could see the hurt in her eyes, the disappointment.

"We can't," I repeated.

"You said that," she said as she reached out to touch my arm.

I pulled back which made her wince and stare at me like I'd hit her.

"If we don't stop, you know where this is going."

"Yes, exactly," she said as she stepped towards me.

"We can't. You'll end up pregnant."

"Tanner Parks, being responsible," she said in half jest. But I could see it in her eyes, the hope that I would change my mind.

Taking a deep breath I said, "I'm doing it for the woman I love."

She stared at me for a long moment then melted into my arms, holding me, her arms squeezing me as if I was the last rock in a raging river.

"I love you too," she whispered into my chest.

She let out a long breath then stepped back and reached up to caress my cheek. "Okay, I understand."

"You're not mad at me?" I asked her.

"I'm furious with you, if you must know. But I understand. And you're right. But I am mad at you for being right."

I did not roll my eyes. It was hard not to, but I was learning.

Britney started crying from inside the tent, giving us a reason to break this tension. Haley went in to take care of the baby. She came back out a few minutes later, changed. She was now wearing long pants and her shirt was untied.

She caught me looking at her and said, "Shut up." But she said it with a smile that let me know we were okay.

After dinner, we both sat with our backs to the bank and watched the fire dance.

"This changes things," she said as she leaned over and nudged me with her shoulder.

"Yes, it does," I replied, nudging her back.

"What do you see changing," she asked me after a moment.

"Well, for one thing, I figure when we get to your grandfather's farm. I might stick around."

Slapping my arm she shook her head, "Don't count your chickens. No one has invited you."

Smiling, I leaned over and kissed her then said, "Be careful or I might find me a new woman on the way."

Her eyes grew suddenly very serious. "No, you won't. Not you. You wouldn't hurt me like that."

Smiling, I sighed as I leaned my forehead next to hers. "You're right. Besides, When a guy finds the best girl possible, he doesn't risk anything that could ruin it."

She buried her head in the crook of my shoulder and said, "I love you."

My soul ached with pure happiness. In my entire life, I had never expected a girl like Haley to fall for me. I mean she was smart, beautiful, kind, peaceful, everything a guy could want.

"I will love you forever," I whispered back, and once again we came together. And once again I stopped us from going too far.

I will never forget that night, our shared happiness. It was as if I had found the missing part of my soul. But alas, the sun rises, and a new day comes upon us. Once more we took to the river. But things were different, Haley was constantly looking back at me over her shoulder. Sometimes with doubt, as if she expected me to disappear into thin air. Other times with obvious love. When we stopped for lunch, Haley couldn't stop herself from touching me, brushing her fingers along my arm. Pushing the hair out of my eyes, tugging at my beard.

All I could do was smile back at her and force myself not to take her there and then. We'd never make Idaho.

For the next four days, it was like that. This unbelievable tension but this sweetness filled with hope. Britney and Jordan were part of our world, but everything else was gone. I'd scavenge gas when we needed it, fish the river, but mostly, I moved us west, as fast and far as possible.

The only problem we had was in the Missouri Breaks area of Montana. Forty miles of nothing but rocky cliffs, barren hills, and the occasional ranch. The air had a dusty smell. So different than New York City.

At midday, we passed a rider sitting on a horse up on a ridge. A rifle across his lap. Watching us until we curved around a bend.

I was worried that we would run out of gas before we broke out the other end. But thankfully, we came across a boat tied off to a stump with two huge outboard engines. "So modern, so big," I said as I pulled in closer my eyes scanning the bank for the boat's owner. "They must have failed after the EMP. The people probably had to hike out of here."

Haley nodded as she helped me keep a sharp lookout. But twenty gallons of gas was too valuable to pass up. Ten minutes and we were out of there.

The countryside was different. Isolated, wilderness. No more farms. Twice we passed through small towns that looked like they only had a couple hundred people. My building in New York had more tenants.

But something pulled at me. I don't know, but I sort of was beginning to feel at home. Like I'd finally found the place I belonged.

Either that, or it was because Haley liked it and the world just seemed perfect.

Later that night, Haley turned over in her sleeping bag all the way on the other side of the tent. If we didn't keep distance between us, I wouldn't be able to keep my hands to myself. She smiled at me then said, "We should hit Fort Benton tomorrow. We need to stop."

"How do you know where we are at? I mean, it's not like google maps is working."

She laughed then shrugged. "I always liked maps. I sort of just remember. I know where the "Breaks" are. Fort Benton is just beyond that."

"How far do we have to go before we switch to roads? The river doesn't go all the way, does it?"

She shook her head. "I think Helena if we can get that far. There are a couple of dams. Maybe two or three days. We need to catch highway 12 then over to 90. Then there is the minor detail of walking over the Rockies."

Sighing, I nodded as my gut turned over at the thought of what I might run into when we were walking. The river had protected us in so many ways.

"We need to stop in Fort Benton though."

"Why?"

"Lots of things. Baby formula, and … other things."

The shy look she shot me let me know what she wanted me to get. I couldn't help but smile as my heart soared. Fort Benton, here we come. I only hoped the drug stores hadn't all been cleaned out.

It was just after ten the next morning when I tied off the boat to a small pier and helped Haley and Britney up out of the boat. I clipped a leash on Jordan and started for town.

The town was quiet, no cars moving, no air conditioners running, just an unusual quiet that set my skin on full alert.

People were out, not scurrying, not afraid, just going about their business. In a park, a group of boys were playing baseball. "Things can't be too bad," I said to Haley. She looked at the boys and nodded.

"Farms, Ranches," she said, "They're not hurting for food." But we kept close as we walked through the town then Haley grabbed my hand and pointed to a drug store.

We were almost there when I realized I'd never let go of her hand. God, we must look like a newlywed family. Smiling at her, my heart melted until I pulled myself back to reality. We were in a strange town at the end of the world. I shouldn't be losing focus like that.

Miricle of miracles, the store was open, And looked like it hadn't been cleaned out. Two storm lanterns threw enough light to see the shelves still had some things. Wow, these people were remaining civilized. I thought of all the problems we had on the way.

I reached to pull the door open when a voice barked, "Freeze, don't move."

My entire body tensed as I turned to find a grizzled cop with his hand on his gun staring at me like I was a serial killer after his kids.

Being the smart person I am, I dropped my hand off the handle and stepped between him and Haley.

"I said freeze," he barked as he pulled his gun halfway out of his holster.

God, the guy looked like a central casting cowboy, the hat, grizzled beard, boots, gun. It might be a hundred years since the west was won, but you couldn't tell by looking at this guy.

I slowly lifted my hands to let him know I wasn't a threat. Especially keeping them far away from the pistol tucked into my belt.

He examined me and I could see it in his eyes. A big man who could probably take him in about two seconds. I bet anything he wished he could call his buddies for back up.

"You ain't from around here," he said as his eyes narrowed. "How'd you get past the check point?"

I shrugged, making sure to keep my hands in clear view. "I don't know about this check point. We came in on the river."

His eyes grew large as he realized there was a back way into his paradise.

"We just want some things," Haley said, peeking out from around me. "Baby formula."

The cop frowned as he inspected Haley and the baby then back at me. I could see the conflict. We were strangers, we were a threat to their resources. Resources needed by their children. But we had a baby. Babies were innocent and needed to be protected.

"We'll get what we need," I said. "Then be on our way. We won't even stay the night."

His eyes narrowed as he studied me for a long moment. "How you going to pay? They ain't taking money. Credit cards ain't working. And we shoot looters. That includes shoplifters."

My stomach clenched as I realized the man wasn't joking. If I gave him an excuse he'd shoot me and never feel a twinge of guilt.

"Maybe we can trade," I said, holding my breath. "But we need to go in and see if they've got what we need."

He studied us for a long moment then Britney turned in Haley's arms and smiled at the man. I swear it was like she wrapped him around her little finger. He sighed heavily then nodded for us to go in. But he shot me a look reminding me to be careful.

Swallowing, I held the door for Haley and the baby, but I could feel his eyes boring into my back, waiting for an excuse to shoot me.

Chapter Twenty

Haley

As we entered the drug store, Tanner put out a hand to stop me as he stepped in front, stopped, then scanned the store, obviously looking for danger.

A warmth filled me. The man I loved was always protecting me and Britney. Of course, I got all gooey inside. The small giant was my pet monster. It made me feel safe, secure, special, loved, all rolled up in one. But it also made me feel feminine, small, and treasured.

Two storm lanterns threw a yellow light filled with shadows. The shelves were not bare, but I didn't see any baby formula. My heart fell as a fear filled me.

"Can I help you," A youngish guy said from behind the counter. Long hair in a ponytail. Tall, skinny.

"Baby formula, the powder kind," Tanner said.

The guy winced and shook his head. "We sold out the first day. Mrs. Andrews came in and bought every can, paid cash. Not one of my smarter moves. The cash is useless now."

Tanner growled deep in his throat. "Where does she live? Maybe she'll trade us some."

The guy shook his head. "She's got twins. About the same age as your daughter. We didn't have much, maybe ten cans."

"What about other stores?" I asked, "The hospital?"

He scoffed. "We don't have a hospital, a clinic mostly. And I'm pretty sure everywhere is picked over. It's been two weeks."

My heart skipped a beat as I tried to figure out what we were going to do. A baby needed to eat. Glancing over at Tanner I saw a determination in his eyes that told me he realized just how bad it was.

"We'll check out the other stores," Tanner said as he started me for the door.

I was so upset I didn't even think about the other things I had wanted him to get. All I could think about was Britney.

The cop was gone when we got outside. Tanner scanned the area then pulled me down the street. "We'll find some," he said.

Unfortunately, we didn't. Every store, church, every doctor's office, nothing. Each disappointment was like an arrow to my heart.

"We've got about a week's worth," Tanner said when we realized there was no one else to ask. "And if we start giving her mashed-up regular food, we can stretch it to ten days. Maybe we'll be at your grandfather's by then.

I cursed, "What good will that do? It's not like he's got a cellar full of baby formula."

"It's a farm," Tanner said. "They should have a cow, right?"

It took effort to not roll my eyes. "It's not the same thing."

Tanner shrugged, "We'll keep looking on our way. There's got to be towns along the way.

All I could do was look at the baby in my arms and feel helpless. She was my responsibility. Nothing else was more important.

We got back to our boat and traveled another ten miles up the river to stop just before dark. Tanner made camp while I changed Britney then introduced her to mushed mandarin oranges. I know, but I didn't have a lot to choose from.

As I was feeding her, I felt a sense of failure. This wasn't right, not fair. She deserved so much more, real baby food, out of jars. A mother who lived, or at least someone who knew what they were doing.

We stopped in every little town along the way. This was western Montana, not a very crowded place. No luck. Each day, I measured out more formula and felt my gut tighten.

We were able to score three pounds of oatmeal in Great Falls. No formula, but every calory counted. Tanner traded the folding buck knife he'd taken off the man who'd cornered me.

We were about a day out of Helena when I told Tanner we were going to have to leave the river and start for the mountains. His eyes grew big then he took a deep breath and nodded.

"We'll scour Helena then start for Idaho," he said. "We'll find something."

I grimaced but didn't tell him how frightened I was. Things had changed between us. I was just too worried about Britney to feel close to him. Oh, I still loved him. I always would. But I couldn't think about myself. Besides, he hadn't found any protection, so I didn't have to worry.

Although, there were times I just wanted to crawl into his arms and forget about this new world. Become lost in loving him. But then Britney would fuss and I would be reminded of what was important and feel guilty for not putting her first always.

Helena had almost thirty thousand people but no formula. We hit every store, anything we could think of. We returned to the boat empty-handed. We'd camp that night on the river then start our hike in the morning.

Later, after the stars were out, Tanner built up the fire then started laying out all of our gear on a blanket.

"What are you doing?"

He shrugged, "figuring out what we take, what we leave. I can hump about sixty pounds. Seventy if I have to."

"I can take some."

"No," he snapped then said, "I'm sorry, but you've got Britney and the diaper stuff. That's enough."

I was going to argue with him, but Britney started fussing. She'd been doing that a lot lately which made me freak out. I was positive it was the solid food I was giving her. But what could I do?

"How did they do it?" I asked as I rocked the baby. "I mean in the olden days."

Tanner shook his head, and I knew what he was thinking. Half of babies never made it to their first birthday in the olden days. The thought turned my insides to pure jelly.

"We'll figure it out. Get some sleep. She won't settle down until you're both tucked into your sleeping bag."

I smiled at him, he knew her. God, I was so lucky, what would have happened if he hadn't saved me that first day? I never would have made it this far. I never would have found Britney. Without me thinking, a tear formed in the corner of my eye. I turned away so he wouldn't see in the firelight. No way did I need to burden him with my silly emotions.

The next morning I woke to find Tanner already up, cooking breakfast. "Eat up," he said when I stuck my head out of the tent. "I'm cooking up all the canned food we're not taking with us." He then pointed to his pack stuffed to the gills. "I'll tie off the tent across the top and your sleeping bag and two blankets on the bottom."

I glanced at the pile we'd be leaving. Clothes, extra blankets, a Dutch over, four empty water bottles. Other things we'd picked up along the way. My heart fell, we had so little, and we were leaving half of it behind. Letting out a long breath, I nodded. Of course we had to leave it, we needed to walk over the Rockies.

After breakfast, he clipped the leash to Jordan then shouldered his heavy pack and held Britney while I swung the small diaper pack onto my back. Then giving me back the baby we started for the mountains.

"We take highway 12 to catch I-90."

He just nodded, bent under the weight he gave me a quick smile trying to reassure me. I glanced at his pack and the way it hung on him and just knew he'd packed over eighty pounds into it. I mean the man was a giant, but he was going to have to walk twenty miles a day carrying that weight. Most of it uphill.

As we worked our way through Helena we would see people, some were putting in gardens. We even saw some idiot mowing his

219

grass with a push mower. A pristine lawn. I could only shake my head. Some people's priorities would never make sense.

We had almost reached the edge of town when A sheriff on an appaloosa horse stopped us. He sat up there, tilting his hat to keep the sun out of his eyes while he examined us. Tanner told him where we'd come from and what we were doing.

"New York," the man said as he shook his head. "That is a bit. Not many would have made it this far."

"Yes sir," Tanner said as he sort of puffed up. A little. I felt proud when I saw the respect in the sheriff's eyes. That's right, I wanted to say. My boyfriend is special. Rough, tough, and sweeter than sugar.

The sheriff touched his hat in salute then pulled the horse to the left to finish his patrol. We weren't an issue, we were leaving.

Tanner took a deep breath then started up the road. I hurried to catch up with him. I was realizing that once he started going he didn't like to stop. I guess getting all that weight moving in the right direction took effort.

Once we left town the country changed to rolling brown hills, dry, dusty, small bunches of pine and cedars, with the occasional creek bottom and cottonwood. The air smelled of sage and dust with a west wind hinting at rain.

Slowly, the hills turned to upward slants leading to the mountains.

Tanner bent under his pack, focused on the road. I held Britney or used the sling he'd made for me all the way back east. It seemed so long ago. We only made about ten miles that first day. Uphill and further away from people.

We stopped by a creek and Tanner gave a huge sigh when he slipped the pack off his shoulders and let it down with a thud. Following it to the ground to sit next to a fallen tree. A deep V of sweat told me just how hard he had worked to get this far.

Curious, I reached over to lift his pack and couldn't budge it, I swear it had to be over ninety pounds.

"You can't carry that all the way to Idaho. We have to go over mountains."

He just stared at me then shrugged. "There's nothing in there I think we can leave behind."

All I could do was roll my eyes then hand him the baby. "Hold her," I said, "I'll get things set up."

He didn't fight me, just held Britney, nuzzling her neck while he regained his strength. I had the tent up and my sleeping bag rolled out. "Where's yours?" I asked him as a sick feeling filled me.

He laughed, "I don't need one. I can get by with a blanket."

"Tanner," I scoffed. "This is the mountains. It will get cold at night, especially this time of year."

He shrugged then let Briney pull at his ear.

I could only shake my head. It was too late. We weren't walking back for it. So I solved my concern by opening my bag all the way and spreading the two blankets over it. "We're sleeping next to each other. And don't you dare turn me away."

He looked at the pallet I'd built then at me and shook his head. "You're lucky I'm so tired."

"Lucky, or cursed," I mumbled under my breath.

Chapter Twenty-One

Tanner

I woke up the next morning with my arm wrapped around Hailey, my body stiff from carrying all that weight uphill. I swear every muscle ached, screaming to be rubbed.

But I refused to move, just enjoying holding Hailey.

"Good morning," she said as she snuggled back into me and sighed heavily.

Cursing to myself I rolled away from her and pushed myself up. If I didn't, I'd never have left her alone and we'd have been stuck there for the next two weeks.

She pouted, shooting me upset looks but I ignored her and hobbled outside to start a fire.

An hour later we were on the road, uphill. Always uphill. The air smelled of pine and dust. The road rose up through the mountains or at least what I thought were mountains. Later that afternoon we crested the mountain we were on, and I could look out to the west and see an endless series of mountains like a saw's teeth stretching forever.

My heart sank and my back screamed in anguish but all I could do was take a deep breath and focus on moving forward.

As we came down out of that first set of mountains the country changed again, brown with green patches along the creeks.

There were cars, empty cars, every mile or so and I knew they'd get thicker when we hit I-90. I wondered what happened to all the people. It had been two weeks. Surely, they had had time to make it to civilization.

But what then? Had the towns taken them in? Like us, they'd be homeless. But at least we had a destination. A place to go to. Had they walked home? Had they made it? And what then? A thousand thoughts tumbled through my mind as I tried to focus on ignoring the pain in my back.

That night we camped just past an empty truck stop, next to the Blackfoot River. Really more like a creek if you ask me. I mean, I'd been on the Hudson, Mohawk, the Erie canal, Ohio, Mississippi, and Missouri, I had become an expert on rivers. Believe me, this was more a creek. Bigger than a stream, smaller than a river.

The truck stop was dark and empty. I was tempted to break in and search for food, but I saw the door was already smashed and hanging on one hinge. If there had been food, it was long gone. So I moved us about a mile down the road.

Later that night I woke to Haley pushing at my back, hissing, "Tanner, Tanner."

I forced myself to wake up to hear Jordan growling deep in his throat. A strange, almost hesitant growl, not an angry growl, more a terrified growl.

"What is it," I asked him as I gently petted his back.

He looked at me with a silent thanks then froze when a wolf's howl broke the night's silence. A soul-searing sound that plucked at my primordial fears.

I'm no Daniel Boone type, but that sounded close. Way too close.

Haley instinctively scooped up Britney then looked at me with wide eyes.

It was the second howl, just as close but in the opposite direction, that made me flinch. I retrieved my pistol from under my jacket and started to open the zipper.

"Don't leave," Haley hissed.

"I'm just stepping outside to see if I can see anything. Keep Jordan here."

She wrapped an arm around my dog's neck then said, "It's safer in here."

I almost laughed at her, I mean a tent wasn't keeping anything out. But I had grown smarter and kept my mouth shut and just went outside.

The night was dark with a heavy cloud cover, no moon, no stars. Darker than an elevator shaft. Man, I could be attacked and never see it coming I realized as a shiver shot down my back.

"Tanner?" Haley called.

"I'm here," I said to her. "I'm going to start a fire. Animals don't like fires. Right?" I stirred up the embers and used some tinder to get a new flame dancing. I'll admit I sort of felt a little proud. Two weeks ago it would have taken half a can of lighter fluid and a box of matches for me to get something going, but two weeks camping out and I was becoming an expert.

Just then that damn wolf howled again, a long, low, howl that made my back teeth ache.

"I'm here," I said to Haley before she could call for me.

She laughed then unzipped the zipper enough to stick her head out. The orange flames gave off just enough light for me to see her beautiful face. "I'd join you, but I don't want to leave Britney."

"Go to sleep," I told her. "I'll stay up for a bit then join you."

She sighed heavily then went back to the baby. I threw another stick on the fire and cursed myself. I'd chosen a campsite on a flat open space. I could be attacked from any direction. And it wasn't only wolves I had to worry about, but mountain lions and grizzly bears.

No, I realized. I needed to treat this place like the worst neighborhoods in New York. Keep my head on a swivel and outthink problems.

I spent that night feeding the fire and didn't really relax until the sun peeked over the mountains behind us.

"Did you sleep?" Haley asked as she opened the tent.

"A bit."

She studied me for a second then shook her head, "You are a terrible liar."

I ignored her as I prepared a pot to boil water. We did that for all of Britney's bottles. We'd purify water in the morning then use it throughout the day. I had done enough so I could also make oatmeal.

Have I told you how terrible oatmeal is without sugar, butter, syrup, or a pinch of salt? It was basically wall paste. But it was fuel, and we were going to need it.

The morning sky exposed a strange gray overcast, heavy, lower than normal. Not that normal big Montana sky. Haley caught me staring up at the sky then shook her head. As we walked, I noticed a gray gritty film covering the road and a thickness to the air.

"I think it's ash," she said with surprise.

I stared at her trying to understand.

"Maybe there's forest fires out west?" she added with a shrug.

"Great," I said, "One more thing to worry about."

The ash covered everything but didn't stop us, we continued walking, again, mostly uphill. Each time we passed a farm or small village I'd check my pistol in my belt then scrunch my shoulders until we were safely past.

Twice we saw people standing outside of their place silently watching us pass, not hostile, but not welcoming either. Of course, I couldn't blame them. They needed to protect what they had, and it was easy to imagine less than savory people on the road. People lost, alone, with no hope.

As we came to the town of Missoula I started to feel a small hope. Maybe we could find baby formula or something to help with Britney but my hopes were shattered as we approached. A small gathering of people were camping out at the edge of the town. Tarps and scraggly blankets. What would have been a homeless camp if it had been in Central Park.

Twenty yards further two policemen stood behind a hay wagon parked across the road.

I held out a hand to keep Haley behind me and approached the people sitting around a campfire. Three groups, maybe a dozen people, including two kids. They didn't look well off. The pot on the fire had a weak stew smell.

"Hello," I said.

A gray-haired man of about forty dressed in a suit jacket of all things frowned at me and stepped between us and the pot on the fire. "We don't got enough to share,"

I nodded, "Understand." Then I glanced at the cops. "They keeping people out? We just want to go through. Going to Idaho."

The man stared at us then said, "Idaho's keeping everyone out. They won't let anyone in.

"No," Haley gasped behind me.

"At least the cops here will escort you through. You can't stay in the town though. And really, why bother? There's nowhere to go."

I looked at the group and wanted to shake my head. Staying here wasn't the answer either. These people looked like they'd given up. I glanced over at the two kids, maybe eight and ten, and my heart broke. Three weeks ago they were going to school and fighting over video games. Now they had a haunted, haggard look of permanent terror.

But true to his word, the cops were willing to escort us through the town and out the other side.

We were about a mile down the road, the youngest cop behind us making sure we didn't dart off the road. "Really," I asked as I glanced over my shoulder. "Are you going to shoot us if we make a run for it into your town?"

He frowned as he shrugged, "Probably."

I rolled my eyes. So much for protecting and serving the public. Although, I guess in his new world we were no longer his public.

Haley reached over and took my hand. I could see the worry in her eyes. She knew me well. I didn't like being told what I could or could not do. I just naturally had the urge to rebel. To push back.

But things were different now, I realized. Haley and Britney made things different. Before if I was hurt, no big deal. I was a big boy and lived with the consequences. But not now. Now their fate rested in my hands. Things I could no longer risk.

Letting out a long breath, I squeezed Haley's hand to let her know she could relax. The smile she gave me made me sigh with happiness. No matter what happened, I had that moment, the love in her eyes.

It took two hours to reach the other end of the town. We were let through a barricade and told not to come back.

"Thanks for the hospitality," I grumbled under my breath loud enough for them to hear. But once more we were on our own. Later that night I found a camping spot with our backs to an L-shaped bluff, a creek flowing in front. After I had the tent up, I moved some logs to protect us from the south.

"It won't stop anything, but it will slow it down and let us know it's there."

Haley smiled then returned to feeding Britney some smushed rice and a stale oriole cookie. She'd separated nine of them out and was going to give the baby one each evening.

A sense of guilt filled me as I thought about what I wasn't doing for the baby. You'd think that finding baby formula wouldn't be that hard. I probably could have found a truck full in New York. I mean anything and everything was available there, at a price.

But out here. There just weren't enough people. The empty space was just so weird. I mean I had grown up surrounded by six million people all within twenty miles. I mean literally. You couldn't sneeze without hitting someone.

This was just so different. Between wolf howls, seeing stars at night, and just the quietness. I wondered if I would ever get used to it.

Haley rocked Britney to sleep before putting her on her blanket in the tent. Coming back out she smiled at me. "She's adjusting to the solid food. It's too early to start weaning her, but we don't have a choice. I'm going to give her two bottles a day. Another of just water, and then a part of our food at each meal.

I nodded, so thankful that Haley knew what she was doing.

"How far to Idaho?" I asked her.

She grimaced and shook her head, "The highway parallels the border for about fifty miles. It crosses over by Mullan. Then about thirty miles to Coeur d'Alene, then forty more miles north. Papa's farm is about three miles past Elmira."

"How big is that town?"

Haley laughed then shook her head. "it's not a town. It's a gas station, a bar, and a church, about twenty people. Papa is up next to the Kanisku National Forest. His grandfather, my great, great, grandfather cut out a hundred and sixty acres for a homestead, harvested the timber a hundred years ago, runs a few cows, a couple acres of corn, and sells off an acre of trees whenever he needs cash."

"Sounds like the perfect spot to be to survive the end of the world."

She nodded. "I worry about my brother, my cousins. We are all supposed to head there. But it seems impossible that we'd all make it."

"Hey, we made it this far," I said to her as I wrapped my arm around her shoulder. She sighed and sank into me. My heart ached, needing her to be safe. A hundred and twenty miles. Please, I prayed, just let me get her to her family. Let me get her to safety. If I could do that, then my life would have been worth something.

Chapter Twenty-Two

<u>Haley</u>

The road seemed endless. Almost always uphill. And Tanner was doing it with ninety pounds on his back. I sighed and glanced up at the gray sky.

The ash clouds were still there, low and menacing. We were rounding a switchback when a strange sound broke the morning silence. Tanner froze, his brow furrowed as he looked at me then smiled as he pulled me off the road.

I had just placed it when an ancient pick-up truck came around the switchback below us, chugging up the mountain. A maroon step-side Ford.

Gawking, I stared, my mouth open, trying to understand what I was seeing. Tanner said, "It's like those outboard engines. So old it doesn't have transistors or things that can be hurt by an EMP. No fuel injection. Just old-fashioned distributor and carburetor."

A small hope flowered deep inside of me. Civilization wasn't completely dead.

The truck came around the bend we'd just finished, an old man in coveralls behind the wheel. He saw us and let the truck come to a halt.

"Hello," Tanner said with a small wave. "Didn't think I'd see something so beautiful ever again."

The man smiled as he patted the side of his door. "Sixty years old and the best thing on four wheels. In fact, the only thing on four wheels that still moves."

Tanner laughed, that male bonding about cars seemed to kick in instantly. "Where you headed?" he asked, and I could see the hope in his eyes. That pack must have weighed a ton.

The old man sighed heavily. "Sorry, I'm just going around the bend. You caught me just before I got home."

Tanner's shoulders slumped as he nodded.

"Where you lot headed," the man asked as he glanced at me and the baby.

"Idaho," Tanner said, "Got family there, a farm."

The old man nodded then said, "Long walk." Then his brow furrowed before he said, "You look like an honest family. Would you want to stop by, for dinner?"

My heart skipped a beat then I remembered how many times we'd been fooled by offered hospitality. I could see Tanner thinking the same thing but without even glancing at me he nodded and said how we'd love to stop by.

"Hop in the back. We'll be there in a minute."

Tanner lowered the tailgate, dumped his pack then held Britney while handing me up. Jordan jumped in and we were off. True to his word, a minute later we were turning off the road onto an ancient dirt track that wove through some trees to break out into a small yard next to a doublewide trailer.

We were getting down when the man introduced himself, "Name is William Mclean, do not call me Bill, or Willie."

Tanner laughed as he stretched out his hand, "Hi, I'm Tanner Parks, this is Haley Conrad, and the little one is named Britney."

The man frowned then shrugged, "I would have thought you two were married, you have that look."

Tanner laughed then shocked me by saying, "We're waiting until we get to her family in Idaho."

My jaw dropped as I stared at him. We hadn't talked about this. He hadn't even asked me. But he was making a big deal about it to this guy.

The man nodded then said, "Well, you're lucky. I've got two spare rooms. Can't have unmarried people sharing a room. Wouldn't be right?

My mind was still whirling as I tried to figure out what Tanner meant and why he had said we were getting married. And why he refused to look at me. All while trying to understand this man's ancient ideas and moral values. Then I realized he'd probably been born when such ideas were common.

Mr. McLean led us into a clean home. I held my breath waiting for a monster to appear. But everything seemed okay.

"Macaroni and cheese?" he asked.

My mouth watered as I vigorously nodded. He started preparing dinner with powdered milk all while asking a thousand questions.

We ended up spending the evening talking about everything, telling him our story. We explored all the ways civilization had disappeared and what we could do instead.

He broke out a bottle of whiskey and gave us each a little then sat down to tell us about being all alone and preferring it that way. He was a retired welder. "Spent the last few years working in the oil fields out in South Dakota. I retired and two months later the world ended." The truck had been his father's. "It works just fine, but once the gas is gone, I'm stuck out here."

"You can come with us," I said before I could stop myself. The thought of being left alone in the wilderness just seemed wrong.

He shook his head. "No, There's deer and Elk, fish in the creek and I might put in a garden. If I stretch it, I've got enough gas to get to town and back six or seven more times."

I saw a sadness in his eyes and realized he was looking at the end of his life and wondering what it had all been for. It made me think. What would I look back on at the end of my life? Would I be pleased and happy with what I accomplished? Would I be leaving a better world?

Glancing over at Britney sleeping on the couch, I felt a determination fill me. I would do one thing in this world or die trying. I would see that baby live to a happy adulthood.

Tanner had been sort of quiet throughout the night. I caught him looking off into the distance. When Mr. McLean left us to go to the bathroom, I poked Tanner and said, "What are you thinking? He seems okay."

Shaking his head, Tanner said, "No, I was realizing how far we have come."

"I know …"

"No," he continued. "Not distance, but us, as people. I mean, you're basically a mom now. I'm responsible for keeping you both alive. And oh yeah, I've sort of fallen in love with you. So some changes."

My heart soared as I heard the authenticity in his words.

"Um, about this wedding we're supposed to have when we get there."

He laughed then sheepishly shrugged. "I sort of forgot to ask you, didn't I?"

"Um, yeah," I said.

He smiled. "Is that yeah in yes you'll marry me, or yeah in you agree I forgot to ask."

Rolling my eyes I slapped his shoulder. "Ask me right, Tanner Parks or I will make your life miserable."

He smiled then said those magic words, "Haley Conrad, will you marry me."

The words had barely left his mouth before I threw myself at him and said, "Yes, a thousand times yes."

Mr. McLean found me sitting on Tanner's lap, hugging him, smiling wide, and shedding tears of happiness.

We spent another hour talking then I got Britney ready for bed. Mr. McLean showed me to my room. I used the bottom dresser drawer for Britney's bassinet. Mr. Mclean watched me get the baby settled then nodded, obviously approving of my maternal skills. He started to close the door then informed me Tanner would be across the hall. I almost laughed at him. Tanner and I had shared a tent for three weeks. But I guess old people have their values and since we weren't married, we couldn't sleep in the same room.

I wanted to roll my eyes, but the man had been so kind, and it was only one night. Unfortunately, as I lay there in that wonderfully soft bed staring up at the ceiling all I could think about was Tanner. My future husband. Every cell in my body demanded I go to him. That we share ourselves.

But doubt filled me. What would Tanner think?

Grinding my teeth in frustration, I punched my pillow and turned to face the door. The silvery moonlight peeking through the window allowed me to see the handle slowly turn.

I held my breath. A thousand fears filled me.

Tanner stuck his head in the door and smiled hesitantly.

Without thinking, I lifted my blankets, silently begging him to join me.

His smile widened as he tiptoed across the room and crawled into bed with me. I won't talk about what happened after that. But in my heart, I considered myself married to the man from that night on.

We left the next morning after a hearty meal of grits with real butter. Mr. Mclean said we had to use it up before it went bad. As we hit the road, Tanner and I held hands, constantly looking at each other and smiling, or worse, breaking out in giggles. Neither of us able to believe how lucky we were.

Of course, nothing lasts, and this new universe was determined to ruin any happiness that might exist. After two days of bliss, we hit the Idaho border at the bottom of a ski resort.

Four men, soldiers, stood behind a barbed wire fence across the road. A fence that looked like it had been hastily installed, running off into the forest on either side. A less welcoming sight is hard to imagine.

All four watched as we approached. Young men in camouflage. Rifles slung over their shoulders. Something told me they were not regular. They looked too young.

Tanner held out a hand to slow me down so he could get in front. I know, his permanent macho way of doing things, but deep down, I didn't mind. It sent a warmth through my body.

"That's far enough," one of the soldiers said holding up his hand.

Tanner sighed heavily as he unshouldered his pack and let it drop to the road with a heavy thunk. "Really?" He said shaking his head. He then pointed to the mountains around us. "You can't keep it all blocked off."

The soldier didn't laugh he just said, "You'd be surprised what we can do. And trying to get in will end up getting you and your family hurt."

"Please," I said stepping around Tanner, making sure the soldiers could see the baby. "We need to get to my grandfather's farm. Just north of Elmira."

The soldier frowned then whispered something to another soldier who ran off to a small shack before returning with a clipboard and several pages fluttering in the wind.

"What's your name," the soldier asked as he studied the papers.

"Haley Conrad," I said. "This is Britney Carson and Tanner Parks. We've come all the way from New York City. You have to let us in."

The soldier didn't even look up as he ran his finger down the first page, shifted to the second then said, "Your name is on the list, You can come in, but the other two can't."

My world slammed to a halt as I tried to understand. "I can't come in without them. Don't be ridiculous."

He shrugged. "I didn't say you had to come in. I only said they can't."

Tanner stopped me from charging the stupid man. If the soldier thought I was abandoning my family, he was crazy.

"Maybe ...," Tanner started.

"NO!" I snapped. "Do not even think it."

He sighed then glared at the soldier. The man with the clipboard winced and nodded for one of his men to unsling his rifle.

"Is there someone we can talk to? An officer?" I asked. Why was I on the list? Had my grandfather pulled some strings? But he was hundreds of miles away. None of it made sense.

The soldier said, "We'll call it in. We've got communications back with the Captain, he's in Mullan. They ran a salt and pepper line all the way back."

Tanner sighed then shifted us back and to the side of the road where we could sit on an embankment and wait. Their communication must be a landline. Someone figured out a way to power a phone. One of those hand-crank things you used to see in the movies.

Shaking his head, he cursed. "Imagine, there was a time when we had instant communication anywhere in the world via satellite, now it's a miracle if we can talk two miles on an ancient piece of technology.

I leaned into him. I knew he was frustrated and just needed to vent.

Luckily within fifteen minutes, a soldier on horseback raced down the road and slammed to a halt just the other side of the fence. Just like the other soldiers, he carried a rifle slung over his shoulder.

He frowned, his forehead creasing as he looked through the fence at me, then Tanner, and finally the baby. "Haley? Haley Conrad is that you?"

I stared back, unable to believe what I was seeing. "Tim? Tim Devo?"

"Wow," he said as he looked at the baby in my arms. "No one told me."

Tanner flinched, "You know him?"

I smiled. "This is Tim Devo, my ex-boyfriend."

I swear the jealous rage that sprang into Tanner's eyes was not the worst thing I've ever seen. "Tim, what are you doing here?" I asked.

"Looking for you. And Cassie. Ryan told me you guys would be coming so I got myself transferred over to this side."

"Ryan?" I gasped. "You saw my cousin?"

Tim nodded, "A couple of weeks ago, just outside of Spokane. Him and some kids. And a pretty girl named Kelsey. But they couldn't get in. So he headed north." Tim stopped and glanced at the other soldiers then shrugged. "He probably crossed over way up north. But I don't know if he made it or not."

"Should we do that?" I asked.

He frowned then shook his head. "It's patrolled too heavily. I wouldn't recommend it."

"Well, I'm not coming in without my family."

Tim thought for a long moment, then examined Tanner, slowly looking him over then shaking his head. "You will never get in along the border. We've got it locked down. If you try, you'll end up in prison or dead."

Chapter Twenty-Three

Tanner

I didn't like the guy. I didn't like the way he refused to let us in. Or the way he looked at me like I was gum on the bottom of his boot. But most of all I despised the way he looked at Haley. Like she should be his.

He stared up at me and I could see it in his eyes. He hated the fact that I was taller, bigger, and worse of all, Haley smiled at me like I was the most important thing in this world.

"Come on Haley," I said as I gently touched her lower back. "We'll think of something else."

She frowned at her friend, looking disappointed.

He cringed then said, "Hey, I don't make the rules."

"No," she said, "You just enforce them."

Ouch.

I smiled at her as I adjusted my pack then took her hand. We'd find a way across. Her friend remained at the fence, his hands on the barbwire, looking like he'd just lost any chance at happiness.

We walked back down the road away from the border. I waited until we were out of earshot then leaned down and whispered. "We'll find a road or something."

246

She nodded sadly then looked back at her friend.

"So," I began. "Ex-boyfriend, huh."

Shaking her head, she said, "I was twelve. It was summer, he was my brother's friend."

"So what happened?"

She scoffed, "Like I said, he was my brother's friend. Once Chase and Ryan found out they put a quick end to it. Plus I was twelve, it didn't mean anything."

"It meant something to him," I told her. "He's still got a crush on you."

She scoffed again then said, "A lot of good it did me."

I didn't say anything, instead taking her hand in mine, silently letting her know I was there.

We found a creek and set up camp. I needed to come up with a plan. Haley fed the last of the formula to Britney then looked at me like her world was ending. My gut tightened. We were screwed.

Unfortunately, things could get worse as we discovered two days later. I found a trail that led to the ski resort inside Idaho. Five miles from where we'd hit the border. No snow, on the lower slopes. We sneaked through the barbwire. I worked us up the clearing and had just come over the top when we were surrounded by four horsemen, all of them wearing camouflage.

I swear it was like they'd been waiting for us. One moment there was nothing but trees and gray skies then suddenly they were there. They caught us before I could do anything. Besides, I had a girl and a baby. It wasn't like I could start shooting.

I wanted to kick myself. The forest was different than New York. In the city and these guys would never have got me. But out here. There was nowhere to hide, and it was too easy to get lost. Every tree looked like the one next to it.

"Drop the pack," their leader said, pointing his rifle straight at my gut.

My insides clenched as I saw the look of fear in Haley's eyes as she reached out and touched my arm. "Don't," she whispered.

Sighing, I dropped my pack. She was right. I couldn't risk it. Not with her standing next to me.

"Now the gun," the leader said pointing to the pistol in my belt.

Using two fingers, I removed my pistol and laid it on my pack then stepped away. One of the riders jumped down, pulled my hands behind my back, and zip-tied them off. An anger burned through me.

So far. We had come so far, overcome so much, every hurdle only to be stopped by four twerps.

"Come on," The soldier said pulling at my bound arms as he stuffed my gun into his belt.

"What about my stuff?" I asked as I looked at my huge pack.

He laughed, "You're not going to need it where you're going." The three others tore my pack apart, throwing my clothes and cooking utensils into the dirt but passing the food out, sharing it equally.

Haley gasped. My gut tightened. No this was impossible. But deep in my soul I knew it was perfectly possible and I was screwed.

They led me over a small mountain and down a sharp valley. Haley followed. Twice I pulled my arm out of his grip to give Haley time to catch up. Finally, they let Haley take his horse. It was either that or spending the night out there.

My captor kept his hand on my tied wrists. Why? It wasn't like I was going to take off without Haley and Britney.

Seven hours later I was pulled into an army camp and dumped in front of a young Captain who looked like he'd woken up angry and the day had just gotten worse from there.

I could spend the next six pages telling you how screwed up everything was. But it basically came down to the fact that I was going to a prison farm. Martial law, which meant no law.

Haley could stay, her name was on the list. And the Captain was nice enough to allow Britney to stay also.

That was how I found myself on the back of a hay wagon with two other guys, all three of us tied off so tight we weren't getting away.

At the last minute, Haley ran up to the side of the wagon and tried to hug me. "I'll be there," she said. "I promise."

"Haley," I whispered as I took in her warmth. "You and the baby get to your grandfather's. I'll find you. North of Emira, right?"

She laughed. "No."

"Haley," I began.

"No," she snapped. "You don't get to tell me what to do. Not about this."

The steel in her eyes told me I was never going to win this argument. I pulled out the only card I had. "Think about Britney. You have to get her to safety. Find your friend, Devo."

She scowled at me and then shook her head. "No, the only safe place for us is with you."

My gut twisted into a knot at the thought of her being helped by anyone other than me. Suddenly, there was a whistle and the wagon lurched as it started on its journey.

"I love you," she said as she tried to run alongside the wagon, her hand on my leg. The other holding the baby.

"I love you too," I answered as my heart broke. I was leaving her all alone. Alone in a world gone to hell.

A soldier put an arm out to stop her. Slowly, her fingers slid off my pant leg. Our eyes locked as tears dripped down her cheeks. The pain in her eyes will haunt me for the rest of my life. No person should ever feel that much pain.

Jordan howled, obviously confused, begging to be allowed to come with me.

Haley stood there until we turned a bend and my world ended. Growling under my breath I pulled at the ropes binding me. Both of my traveling companions slid away from me, giving me room as I struggled to break free.

There were two men up front, a driver and shotgun. Two men followed on horses with rifles drawn, sitting across their laps.

Finally, I gave up and slumped. I would get my chance, I told myself. Just give it time.

But. I guess those soldier boys had learned a few tricks over the last three weeks. That first night, they tied off my legs before they untied me from the iron rings set in the wagon bed. I had to hop to the side of the road where they tied us off to a huge tree.

They fed us a rough gruel and a bottle of water.

You'll get your chance, I kept telling myself as my heart broke. This was the first night away from Haley and Britney.

It took them three days to get to some Podunk town in the middle of nowhere. The sun was setting in the west. The area was in a bowl surrounded by mountains with farm fields filling most of it.

"Dudley," one of my fellow prisoners explained. For the first time, I examined my companions. I'd been so wrapped up in my pain I hadn't been paying attention. The first guy, the one who said Dudley looked about forty, in a rumpled business suit.

"How do you know?" I asked him. If he knew this area maybe he might be helpful in an escape.

He laughed. "I used to make sales calls in Cour d'Alene, had to drive through here every other week."

"How about you," I asked the second guy as I kicked the bottom of his foot. A heavy guy, mid-thirties, with a gut and lost eyes. He didn't even acknowledge me, just stared off into nothingness.

"I'm Jerry Burleson," suit guy said.

"Tanner Parks," I answered then leaned over and whispered, "I'm going to escape. You in?"

He stared at me for a long moment then laughed. "They're going to feed us. Why would I leave food?"

My heart fell. Most of them would see it that way. No, I was on my own. But I knew I wouldn't be here long. I had to get to Haley.

Then the realization that she might not stay in that army camp. What if she tried for her grandfather's? Did I go back to where I left her or go to where she was going? A sharp fear filled me. If I made the wrong decision I might miss her.

Every day I was away from her put her at risk. I was her protector and I couldn't do that chained to the back of a wagon.

A burning hate filled me. How dare these people do this? It wasn't right. We had every right to be here in their precious state. Of course, they made it worse by putting metal shackles around my ankles and a set around our wrists before leading us to a large tent.

"It's too late for dinner," the guard said. "You'll get fed in the morning."

I thought they'd remove our shackles when we got there but instead, they led us inside a large tent. My gut clenched when I saw two long lines of metal bunks each with a man lying on it, shackled to his bedpost. A metal ring was welded to the steel footer. Their shackles locked to the ring.

"What if we need to go to the bathroom," Jerry asked.

The guard laughed, "Not my problem."

No! How had we gotten this bad this fast? The news media would have a field day with this. There would be protests. Of course not now. Now people were more worried about just surviving. How prisoners were being treated didn't concern them. Besides, there was no media.

I thought about pushing him and charging out the door, but a second guard stood there with his shotgun lowered, ready to blast a hole all the way through me.

Sighing, I turned and examined my surroundings. I needed to find its weakness. The tent held twenty-three men. Now twenty-six. I could leave any time, but I would be dragging a metal cot across the field. The guard towers would pick me off.

As the lock clicked closed the guard looked at me and smiled, "Don't think about escaping. You'll be shot as soon as you step outside this tent after dark, or the fence anytime."

My gut tightened. It took every bit of control not to scowl. Even more not to reach over and grab the man by the neck. I knew I could kill him before anyone could stop me. But what then? So instead I pushed my anger down. Tomorrow, I told myself.

"Haley," I whispered. Please be okay. Please. I will come, I promise.

The next morning a guard pulled open the flap and started yelling. He freed us from our bed posts then laughed as we each rushed to the outhouses across the yard.

Men pushed and shoved to get a spot then waddled out of the barracks into a yard. The leg shackles stopped a man from taking a long step, let alone running. The sun wasn't up yet but there was enough light to see that we were the only group. The only barracks.

Another prisoner, an older guy with a scraggly white beard pointed to where I should stand. "They don't feed us until we all get in our spots."

I shuffled to where he pointed as I quietly examined everything, looking for a weakness, a way to get out.

After a quick meal of boiled mush, they led us out to a field, handing each of us a hoe or shovel. And that was how I spent my day, working the ground, getting it ready for planting. It took ten hours for twenty-six men to turn an acre of earth. Something one man in a tractor could do in ten minutes.

The shackles were loose enough to let us work while keeping us from running. Genius, I thought as I sighed inside. They didn't have enough guards to keep us under constant watch. They just needed enough to stop us if we got too far.

We couldn't rebel, couldn't do anything but toil in their fields.

My back was killing me as we shuffled back to the tent and another bowl of mush. "You call this feeding us," I said to Jerry.

He looked down at the blisters in his hand and shrugged. "It beats going without."

I didn't have the energy to get into an argument. My back screamed and I was in good shape compared to most of the other men. Several were moaning in pain, curled up on their bunks. Others stared at nothing, waiting for the guards to shackle them in for the night.

Deciding I better go one last time, I headed across to the outhouses. Coming out I was confronted by a big guy with a nasty scowl. Someone had referred to him as Bill Miller earlier, out in the field. My radar went to full alert. This idiot thought he was the toughest thing around. I could see it. He had built himself a reputation and needed to keep it going.

That was the thing. This place wasn't filled with hardened criminals. This guy wouldn't have lasted ten minutes in Rykers Island. But here, among salesmen and shopkeepers, he thought he was tough.

The other prisoners backed away giving us room.

Shaking my head I decided I was going to give him one chance. "Back off," I said as I moved to get around him.

He shoved at me, both hands hitting me in the chest as he started to tell me who was in charge.

A week's worth of anger burst out of me. He hadn't said a word when I twisted, grabbed him by the arm, and threw him over my hip. But instead of letting him up, I followed him down, my knee landing on his chest, as I held my chains across his throat.

Staring down into his eyes I let him see how close he was to death, held it there long enough to make my point, then backed up and turned my back, returning to my bunk.

Looking back on it, I wish I'd killed the guy, my life would have been so much better.

Chapter Twenty-Four

Haley

No Tanner, my life became a numb pain. No Tanner. How were Briteny and I supposed to survive in this new world? A thousand emotions continually rushed through me as I watched his wagon disappear.

Fear, sorrow, love, terror, repeat. Over and over.

Jordan looked at me with sorrowful eyes as if I had failed him by letting them take Tanner away from us.

It was Britney squirming in my arms that brought me back to this world. I couldn't morn. I couldn't grieve, I had a little baby that needed me. And no milk for her.

"God," I screamed glaring up at the sky as an anger filled me. An anger at the world, God, the army, the state of Idaho, and anything else I could think of.

"You're alive," I reminded myself. So many weren't so lucky.

Find Tim, Tanner told me. He was my only chance. Sighing, I began to look around. Two dozen tents lined up in a grid pattern, muddy trails between them. A big tent used for a kitchen and another for that evil Captain Tolliver.

"What now?" I asked Britney. I swear things had changed. There had been a time when people, especially the army, would have looked at me as a victim and bent over backward to fix my problems. Now? Nothing.

Gritting my teeth, I started back to the Captain's tent. When he saw me coming his brow furrowed as he shook his head. "Don't even start," he growled as he looked up from a map.

"How could you do that? We weren't hurting anyone." I said to him. "You might have signed my baby's death warrant."

Tilting his head he studied me for a long moment then scoffed. "Don't you think I know what I did? But what choice do we have? If we don't keep people out, we will be overrun. It is still early. A month from now there will be thousands trying to get in. People always run to the mountains in times of famine."

I could only glare at him.

He sighed heavily then shrugged and I realized I had been dismissed. My problems were inconsequential in his world. I was only one of countless victims. "You are authorized to be here. I suggest you use that privilege and find family to be with. Even if you do, it might not be enough, but it might help."

"Family," I cursed as anger shot through me. "You just sent my family to your prison."

Again he shrugged before turning his back on me.

Growling under my breath, I stomped off, half numb. Things were so different. There was no one I could call for help. No one to turn to. It was just Tanner and me against the world and now he was gone. It was as if I had lost half of myself. The better half.

I was weaving my way through tents, numb, half dead when someone called my name. My heart jumped hoping it was Tanner only to turn and see Tim rushing towards me.

"I just heard," he said, half out of breath, "I was up north when I got back, they told me what happened."

Staring up at him I could only feel an emptiness. He was on their side, I reminded myself.

He wrapped an arm around my shoulders then began to pull me to the back of the camp. I allowed myself to be led, numb to the pain.

Britney studied this new stranger, obviously wondering where Tanner was and who was this replacement.

Finally, I could take it no more and sank to my knees as the tears started. Gasping for breath I cried like no woman has ever cried before. No woman had ever lost someone so perfect as my Tanner.

Poor Tim looked at me like I was a basket case. A blubbering, helpless basket case, too crazy to understand.

I didn't care and let myself lose it. I knew other soldiers were looking, I didn't care. Britney was whimpering, I didn't care. I just had too much pain that had to get out.

Somehow, after long minutes, Tim got me up off my knees and into his tent. I wiped at my eyes and examined my surroundings. Four cots, sleeping bags, and a large wooden box painted olive green.

Jordan went to each cot, sniffing at them.

"I'll make the other guys crash somewhere else," he said as he helped me down onto a cot.

Suddenly he left me alone. I could only stare into nothingness as I tried to understand what I was going to do. Unaware of anything.

He returned a few minutes later with a plate of food and a bowl of smashed yams for the baby. "Here," he said as he handed me the plate. As if the food would fix all my problems.

Britney perked up at the smell of the cooked food and I knew she was hungry. The only reason she hadn't whined and whimpered was because I had been doing enough of that for the both of us.

It is amazing how having a baby depending upon you limits your ability to wallow in your misery. They don't care. If you don't feed them, they die.

As I spooned in some of the yams I looked over at Tim, "She needs baby formula."

He cringed, "Not a lot of that in an army camp."

The anger burst out of me. "Well, find some. If you really want to help me. Find some baby formula. Either that or give me back my Tanner. He will save us."

The pain in Tim's eyes didn't impact me in the slightest. I didn't care.

True to his word, Tim made the other soldiers leave me alone in the tent. Just Britney and me.

For the next three days, that became my life. Wallowing in despair while taking care of Britney. Or trying to. No formula meant mushed up food which meant colic and a fussy baby. Poor Britney, she broke my heart. Every time I tried to give her a bottle of water, she would take a few sips then push it away and cry.

My heart would shatter as a sense of failure hit me.

I would take Britney with me to the outhouses they had set up. I made Tim get me two buckets of hot water so I could wash her diapers. Tim would bring us food. But the rest of the time, I would just sit on the edge of the cot and rock back and forth, holding my baby.

The morning of the fourth day, I had just woken, again feeling lost and alone when there was a heavy cough just outside the tent, "Haley?" Tim said, "Can I come in? I've got something for you."

Grumbling under my breath I said, "Fine," with a resigned tone. I really didn't care anymore.

The tent flap was peeled back. Tim stood there with a huge smile and a large can of powder baby formula.

"What? How?" I gasped as my hands reached out to snatch it away from him. Full, unopened.

He grimaced then said, "West of here, just the other side of Mulan, a baby died. They had this left over."

My heart broke. A baby had died. "How did you find out?"

He shrugged, "I've been asking everyone, pestering them constantly. I guess word got around."

I could only stare at the large can in disbelief, then I quickly wrapped an arm around his neck and pulled him down so I could kiss his cheek. "Thank you, you're my hero,"

He stared back at me with wide eyes. Like I'd just made his life worth living.

.oOo.

Tanner

I pulled the hoe through the dirt, piling it up. That was our assignment, make long hills of earth. The older guys would follow us and plant the seed potatoes. Long, stressful labor that ate at my gut. I wasn't going to be here long enough to enjoy the benefits.

There would be no potatoes in my future. Not these. No, I was going to get out of here and back to Haley.

A burning need filled me. Every day away from her and the baby chewed into my soul, taking a part of me away.

How was she doing? It was impossible to imagine the problems she must be facing without me there.

Had she gone to that Tim guy for help? Was she already relying on someone new? The thought tore at me, imagining her with him. I would tell myself that Haley wasn't like that. But deep inside, I doubted it.

I know, not very honorable of me. But what can I say? I was hoeing a field in the hot sun. And it looked like I would be doing it for the rest of my life.

A sadness filled me. I'm usually a pretty even-keeled guy. Forty-Nine to Fifty-One on the emotional scale. But this had thrown me. I felt hopeless, And each day, it only got worse.

Standing up, I pushed at my lower back and took a moment to scan the area. Twenty-six men working the field. Three guards, all on horseback, all with rifles drawn and ready. In the distance a single chain link fence with barbed wire.

An eagle cried as it circled off to the left. My heart broke, envious of his freedom.

Any other time, a minimum security facility. I could have gotten out easily. But these damn shackles on my arms and legs were too much to overcome. I'd tried everything. And I'm a big guy, most things just break when I put my heart into it. But not these. The chains were too strong, the cuffs too thick. The metal ring at night too durable.

I'd worked on my bunk at night, twisting and pulling at the ring but I just couldn't get the leverage I needed. If I got to the other side of the fence, maybe I could get far enough away to cut through the chains. But the bunk ring was too strong. As if they knew what they were doing.

Sighing heavily, I went back to pulling the hoe, heaping the earth. A fear filled me. Was I becoming too complacent? Was I giving up too quickly? Haley, and Britney, both needed me.

I slammed the hoe into the ground and grumbled under my breath. No, I wouldn't give up. I would find a way. Somehow, I would find a way.

When I came to the end of my row I stood up and rolled my shoulders while looking around. The other men were finishing up. I noticed Bill Miller glaring at me. The man didn't have the sense to know when he was outmatched. I swear, if he got a chance, he'd put a shovel upside my head or a knife into my back.

Ignoring him, I got in line for the long walk back to the tent. Twenty-six men shuffled with their shackles clanking and clinking. We got back and were given a few minutes to clean up then served our second helping of mush.

After our crappy dinner, we were allowed to lounge around for a bit before they locked us down for the night. I was lying on my bunk my hands behind my head staring up at the cloth ceiling, going over possible escape scenarios for the thousandth time when one of the guards yelled, "Parks." As he indicated I should follow him.

Frowning to myself I wondered what I'd done now. But I didn't really care, what were they going to do to me, put me on a potato farm and make me work all day?

I bent to get through the tent flap then stood up and froze.

There, across the yard was Haley. My Haley, holding Britney, smiling at me, making the world seem perfect.

Unfortunately, that idiot Tim Devo stood behind her. Looking like he'd kill anyone that messed with her. He'd taken my job.

Chapter Twenty-Five

Haley

My heart broke when I first saw him. His eyes looked hollow. Like he'd been carrying the weight of the world on his shoulders for so long. Then he saw me, and everything changed. It was as if a spark had ignited a bonfire. One simple little thing and he was happy.

He smiled and my world came back into focus.

"Tanner," I whispered as I stepped towards him.

Tim put a hand on my shoulder, stopping me.

Tanner focused on that hand and a monster flared behind his eyes. A small part of my soul soared. Tanner, my Tanner, still loved me. I could see it in the way he looked at me. The way he glared at Tim.

I twisted out from Tim's grip and rushed across the yard to him, Britney on my hip.

He started to reach to pull me into a hug then saw the chains between his wrists and was reminded where he was.

I didn't care and wrapped him in a hug. "They made us tie Jordan up outside of the camp."

"Hey," one of the guards yelled, shaking his head.

Tanner took a deep breath then stepped back. "Don't give them a reason to send you away."

My heart broke as I nodded. He was right.

"How are you?" he asked with obvious concern. "Britney?" here he reached out to caress her cheek.

The baby giggled then grabbed at his chains, breaking his heart.

I sighed. "We're fine. Now that we know you're all right."

He smiled, staring at me, his eyes scanning up and down then over my shoulder to Tim. The anger in his eyes made me gasp.

"Tim got us here," I told him. "A supply run. We came in a wagon. And he found a can of formula. We should be good for another month."

Tanner glared at him then took a deep breath and said, "You shouldn't come here. You should be at your grandfather's."

"No," I said as an anger flared inside of me. Why did he want to send me away? No, I belonged close to him. "NO!" I repeated. "I found a place in town. An empty house. Tim said he'd set me up with some food. Enough to keep us going until I can figure out how to get more."

Tanner glared at Tim and shook his head. "If you cared, you'd get her to her grandfather's."

Tim sighed then said, "It's too far. I've already stretched the rules just helping her this much."

"Screw your rules," Tanner yelled as he took a step towards Tim. My heart jumped. The man was the size of a small mountain and would destroy anyone he got his hands on. Without thinking, I stepped between them and put my hand on his chest, stopping him from doing something we couldn't get away from.

"Tanner," I said, forcing him to see me. "Tim has bent over backward helping us. I couldn't have gotten here otherwise."

Tanner growled deep in his throat. Finally, he brought his beast under control then pulled me away from Tim, and leaned down to whisper, "Where is your house, I will find you. Somehow."

He didn't want Tim to know he was going to escape. It never crossed my mind that he couldn't but then I saw the guard with the rifle staring at us and my heart fell. "No," I said, "they will kill you."

Tanner growled deep in his throat and said, "Tell me."

I could see it in his eyes, this was not something I could talk him out of. "A small white ranch house on Dupont Street." I whispered, "The third on the left. Just west of here."

He sighed then smiled at me, forgiving me for not trusting him. "A couple of days," he whispered as he leaned down close, his breath tickling my cheek.

Britney grabbed his beard and pulled him down with one hand while reaching for him with the other, obviously wanting to be held.

Tanner took her from me and cradled her in his massive arms, rocking her as he smiled down at her making baby sounds.

My heart melted, he loved her so much. Then those awful chains rattled, and I was reminded of where we were and what they were doing to him. An anger filled me. An anger at the world for all it had done to us.

Reaching up, I held his arm as he played with the baby, I just had to be touching him. My rock in a raging river.

Suddenly he pulled back from Britney and glanced over my shoulder. His scowl made me freeze.

"Is your friend staying at the house?"

I could see the jealousy in his eyes and almost laughed. "It's not like that," I assured him.

He scoffed, "Haley, you are a beautiful girl. It is always like that on the guy's side. We can't be trusted. Believe me."

Sighing, I shook my head. "Tanner, don't worry. I'm in love with you, remember? He's the one who talked them into letting me come see you. Besides, he has to go back to his army camp."

Tanner continued to glare for a minute then let his shoulders relax as he focused back on me and the baby.

We spent the next ten minutes just being together, lost in our own little world. Tanner was tickling Britney's cheek when I noticed another prisoner, a big man staring at us with pure hate.

"Who is that?" I asked before I could stop.

Tanner twisted then growled deep in his throat. "Don't worry, he's nothing."

Before I could ask more questions, one of the guards said, "That's enough. Time to go."

Tanner let out a long breath then said to Tim, "Get her a gun. She shouldn't be left alone without one."

Tim nodded.

I reached up to pull Tanner's face back to look at me, "I love you," I said as I pulled him down so I could kiss him.

We kissed, the kiss of a couple, a couple that knew they would be together again. The world could not keep us apart.

Finally, he pulled back and I could see it in his eyes. The resignation. He had to steel himself for what was coming. The loss of freedom, the pain of hard labor, the separation from what he loved. All of it was reality returning to him.

"I'm sorry," I said as guilt filled me. Guilt at being safe on the outside while he was stuck in that hell. Guilt because we were only there because of me. He had been perfectly safe in New York.

"Come on," the guard said as he pulled at Tanner's arm. I almost laughed, the guy pulled, and Tanner didn't budge.

It was like trying to move a mountain. Instead, Tanner caressed my cheek and said, "I will always love you." Then before I could respond, he turned and left me there.

My heart broke as I cried watching him walk away. Tim came up behind me and gently touched my shoulder.

I was tempted to turn to him, to bury my head in his chest and cry. But Tanner didn't deserve to see that. Instead, I sniffled, got myself under control, and forced myself to say. "Let's go home. I need to be there when Tanner comes."

.o0o.

Tanner

It took every bit of my soul not to punch something. Anything. I swear as I stepped into the tent, I was looking for something to destroy when the stupidest man in the world, Bill Miller, yelled "Pretty girlfriend. I'll be sure to look her up when they let me out this weekend."

I flew over three cots to get to him and took about two seconds to get him down on the ground with my hands around his throat. If a guard hadn't cracked me upside the head with a rifle butt I would have killed him.

Sometime in the middle of the night, I returned to this world to discover myself on my bed, my leg irons locked down. Just like every night.

My head pounded like someone was digging a tunnel through solid granite with jackhammers.

Jerry leaned over from the cot next to me and said, "Welcome back to the living. You okay?"

I grunted, it hurt too much to think. The last thing I could remember was my hands around Miller's throat trying to get my fingers to meet in the middle. "Miller?" I asked. Slightly worried I might have killed him. Upset that I might not have.

Jerry hesitated for a moment then said, "They let him out early."

"What?" I gasped.

He shrugged, "They let him out. They were going to have to do it in a couple of days. He was doing six months, got moved here from

274

country jail, I guess. They let him go so they didn't have to worry about keeping you two apart."

I slumped back onto my cot as I tried to understand. Somehow, I had gotten a couple of days knocked off Miller's sentence. That was so my world now.

Closing my eyes, I tried to ignore the pain shooting through my head when I remembered Haley's visit. And Miller's words. NO! No, he didn't know where she was. Did he? No.

A new sickness filled me as I pulled at the ring holding my leg shackles. A feeling of hopelessness washed through me. Of being stuck. Of being a failure.

There had to be a way. There just had to be.

It took me three days to find it. And I could have kicked myself for being such a dunce to have missed it. We were coming back from the fields when I spotted them. The tie-down spikes for the tent.

They'd used rebar, bent at the top. The kind used for concrete. I quickly scanned the area, one guard up front, the other in back. The third had disappeared. When the first rounded the corner, I turned to Jerry and said, "Punch me."

He frowned, looking at me like I'd lost my mind.

I didn't really have time to wait for him to figure it out so I pushed at his chest, knocking him back a step.

Still, he looked at me like I'd gone insane.

"Punch me," I hissed then pushed him again.

He continued to frown then as I reached to push him again, he swung, catching me on the chin.

Not the best punch. In fact, he might have broken his finger, but I didn't care as I went down, rolling in next to the tent.

The guard cursed as he spurred his horse forward placing the horse between Jerry and me rolling on the ground.

While the guard was busy keeping the terrifying Jerry off me, I was working the tent stake out of the ground. Like I've said in the past, I'm a big guy and things tend to move when I work at them.

I was able to slip the tent strap off the stake then work the eighteen-inch bar out of the ground and up into my sleeve without the guard seeing.

A burst of joy filled me when I realized I'd gotten away with it. Pushing myself up, I hurried back into line. I knew some of the other prisoners had seen what I had done. And there was the glaring evidence of a portion of the tent flapping in the wind where I'd freed it from its stake.

But the guard was focused on Jerry, keeping us separated.

I hurried around the corner of the tent, praying the guard wouldn't see the evidence I had left behind. Either that or recognized the metal bar I was hiding.

Please, I prayed, give me this one chance. That is all I ask.

As if in answer to my prayer, it started to rain. That thick heavy rain. The prisoners scurried inside the tent. The guards left us to return to their barracks. The single guard tower in the corner of the field keeping watch over us. Hey, it wasn't like we were hardened criminals. Besides the shackles kept us immobile.

I'd done it, gotten away with the first part. I ate dinner with one hand, I wasn't able to bend my other arm and no way was I letting this bar out of my sight.

Jerry leaned over and said, "I'm not going with you. Don't ask."

"I wasn't going to."

He nodded. "I figure in about six months, during the harvest. That is when it will be a good time to leave. We can take enough food with us."

I laughed, "A hundred pounds of potatoes will last about three months. Put you into the middle of winter. What then?"

His face fell as he thought about it then he shrugged. "At least I'll get fed for the next six months. That's more than a lot of people out there are going to be able to say."

I let the matter drop. I needed to do this alone. I had always known I would be alone.

Later that night, I watched the guard padlock my shackles to the ring then move on to the next one. Another guard stood at the doorway with his rifle ready to shoot anyone who caused a problem.

Wait, I told myself, Just wait.

I swear, the next three hours were the longest of my life. Every fiber of my being demanded I get out of there. That I get to Haley and Britney. They needed me.

Finally, I just couldn't take it anymore and pulled out the bar from inside my sleeve. It had been bent into a hook on one end for the tent strap. Sitting up, I stuck the bar through the ring welded to the bottom of my bunk and began to push.

I think I've told you before that things tend to move when I work on them. All I needed was the leverage provided by the bar. The ring began to twist until I snapped the weld clean off at the base.

And just like that I was free. Or at least free from my cot. The shackles and padlock still hung between my ankles.

Jerry sat up then held out his hand.

"Do you want the bar?" I hissed.

He smiled and grabbed my hand to shake it. "Good luck."

I pumped his hand then grabbed my pillow, dropped to the ground, and crawled to the back of the tent where I was able to slip under and out into the rain.

Holding my breath, I froze, expecting a rifle shot and instant death. But nothing. The night was blacker than the inside of a cat. The rain pounded, no wind, just a constant shower of heavy drops.

Ignoring the rain, I hunched over as I scurried away from the tent towards the fence. More a waddle than a scurry. Those shackles slowed a man down. Where was the guard tower? I wondered as I searched through the gloom. I couldn't see it, and If I couldn't see it, they couldn't see me. Right?

God, how I wished I could have run, but those shackles kept me to a slow shuffle. But still, I somehow made the fence then froze to listen and search. Nothing. There were no patrolling guards. Nothing.

Holding my breath, I used the bar's hook to pull the barbed wire down and the strands together, then threw my now-soaked pillow up over the barbed wire. I used that hooked bar to pull me up and over the wire to drop down to the ground on the other side.

My chains rattled and I only cut myself in a dozen places. But I was there, on the other side, free. Now what?

Chapter Twenty-Six

Haley

There is nothing as lonely as a dark house on a rainy night with your man locked away. Britney slept quietly in her makeshift crib. I'd arranged four dining room chairs on their side, making a square. Now that she was crawling, I was terrified of what she might get into.

The only light came from a weak fire. The only light in a dark room. I'd had to use the slats from the wooden fence out back. Prying them off. They were thin enough that I could break them. I swear, I almost laughed, Tanner would have been able to snap the two-by-fours, probably the fence posts.

He would have made a real fire.

Where was he, I wondered as I scrunched down in my blankets. Suddenly I realized that if he was hurt, no one would tell me. He could be lying in some hospital, and I'd never know. A sick feeling of hopelessness filled me. We were so in trouble. I had enough food for three days. Tim might not make it back before I ran out. What then?

A sudden lightning flash was followed three seconds later by a burst of thunder that made me shudder. It was a fit night for neither man nor beast. A mixture of fear and hope continuously bubbled inside of me. I was terrified that Tanner would be hurt trying to escape. Hopeful that he would get free. All while worried that I had no idea what to do if he didn't.

How had I become so reliant on another being? And it wasn't just his size, or the monster in him he kept under control. No, it was so much more. I needed to see him smile. I needed to feel his caress and the way he looked at me. As if I was the most important person in the world.

My tummy fluttered just thinking about him. I missed him so much, it made life difficult and miserable. If it hadn't been for Britney, I don't know what I would have done.

Jordan suddenly lifted his head up from his paws to stare at the door then at me.

My stomach clenched. Tim had been unable to get me a gun before he left, he promised to bring one with him when he returned.

Without thinking, I grabbed the hammer I had used to pry fence slats loose and held my breath. Surely, I was okay. Scoffing, I shook my head. I hadn't been okay since the day of Impact. Not without Tanner protecting me.

Suddenly, Jordan sprang up, barking, his tail whipping back and forth a mile a minute. Not the angry, protective bark. This was the happy, greeting bark. My heart stopped as I watched the front door.

There were three quick knocks followed by the sweetest, manliest voice in the world saying, "Haley?"

Flying across the room, I threw the door open and jumped into his arms. I didn't care that he couldn't get those massive arms around me because of the chains. I didn't care that he was dripping wet. He was there, in front of me. The rain whipped at us, the dark night reminding me that he was on the run.

He was soaked, his wet hair lying across his forehead, water dripping down his face. But his smile let me know he was okay. My heart broke with pure happiness.

I pulled him in and slammed the door closed before once again wrapping my arms around him. "You made it."

He sighed heavily then said, "I promised, didn't I?"

I squeezed him, refusing to let him go, terrified if I did, he would disappear. After half of forever, he pulled back then looked sadly down at his chains.

Smiling, I left him and rushed to the bedroom to return with a pair of bolt cutters. Loppers, my uncle used to call them.

"Where did you get those?" he asked incredulously.

I couldn't stop smiling, knowing I had been right. "I knew you would need them. So. Where does a person find bolt cutters?"

He shook his head as he took them from my hands.

"High School," I answered. "I remembered our janitor was always cutting locks. Kids forgot their combo. Or someone needed a locker searched."

"So you went to a high school and got these?"

A sense of pride washed through me seeing the admiration in his eyes.

"It wasn't hard," I assured him. "I went during the day. No one was there. I had the flashlight Tim left me. I found the janitor's office. And there they were, on the wall. Britney and I grabbed them and came home. I knew you would need them.

He continued to shake his head as he placed the chain between his wrists into the teeth of the loppers then held it in place as he moved to the back and leaned his gut on the long handles. With a heavy grunt, he was free.

Smiling like he'd just won the state championship he leaned over and kissed me. "You are the smartest girl in the world. The most beautiful also. It's almost unfair how great you are."

My heart melted but before I could throw myself at him again, he was busy working on his ankle shackle chain. Once he had mobility, he was able to cut through the cuffs and be totally free.

Rubbing his wrists, he glared at the metal shackles lying in a heap at his feet. I could see the anger and hate in his eyes and sent up a silent prayer to never have him look at me that way. Only when I was sure he had himself under control did I come to him, craving his arms around me.

"We need to hurry," he said as he hugged me.

"But ..."

He shook his head. "We need to go. I won't be taken back to that place."

"No one knows you're here," I said hopefully.

"Your Tim does. He knew I would come here. He might have told them."

I gasped. "Tim wouldn't do that."

He laughed and shook his head. "Honey, I'd sell my soul to the devil himself if it meant I got a chance to be with you."

My heart fell. No, that was impossible. Besides, Tim knew how I felt about Tanner. No. He wouldn't tell them. "We can't go. I won't take Britney out into that storm."

His shoulders slumped as he nodded. "Okay. But let's get everything ready so we can go as soon as it stops raining."

I looked up at him and felt a need building inside of me. "Later," I told him as I took his hand and led him into the bedroom.

.oOo.

<u>Tanner</u>

A sharp sunbeam poking through the blinds woke me the next morning. Sighing, I closed my eyes and absorbed the feeling of being free. Of sleeping next to Haley. Of being in control of my life again.

"We need to go," I whispered as I leaned over to kiss her cheek.

"Nooooo," she moaned as she turned over to crawl into my arms. "Five minutes."

I laughed and held her as I mapped out our immediate future. Finally though, I had to pull away. It was our only chance, if I didn't, we'd spend the next three days in that bed. So, while she took a few extra minutes I changed and fed Britney and had her up on my shoulder to burp her when Haley stepped out.

Gorgeous, wearing my shirt, her hair messed up, sleepy-eyed. The most beautiful woman in the world. She saw me with the baby and smiled. "You are good at being a father."

My heart swelled. "If we don't get going, I might not get this chance for long."

She sighed then nodded. And I've got to say. When Haley makes up her mind. Things get done fast. Within minutes we were on the road. Her backpack was loaded with the baby stuff and the last of her food. A bag of rice, two cans of tuna, and a sleeve of crackers.

I swung her bag up and adjusted the straps. I'd tied a dozen blankets and a blue tarp I found in the garage across the top. Just before we left, I grabbed a dish towel and wrapped it around a butcher's knife from the kitchen, and stuck it into my belt.

"It's not much," Haley said with a scared look in her eyes.

All I could do was shrug and say, "We'll figure it out."

She nodded then hesitated before opening the door. I kissed her head then moved her aside to go out first. If a dozen guards were waiting for me I wanted to be their target. But the place was empty.

The morning was crisp without being too cold. I knew it'd grow to be a muggy scorcher before the end of the day. A high blue sky, wetness from the storm, and a soft breeze from the west. The rain had pushed out the ash that seemed to hang around all the time. I continued to scan the area before I finally let Haley and the baby out.

"This way," I said as I pointed west.

Haley grabbed my hand and looked up at me like I could solve all of the world's problems. A doubt filled me. How could I possibly get her there?

As if reading my mind she squeezed my hand and asked. "Will they find us?"

Laughing I shook my head. "How? I mean, they don't have radios so they can't call ahead. No pictures of me. So no wanted posters. And by the time they did tell anyone we'll be gone. We just need to move faster than they can."

Her eyes clouded. "But what if someone stops us? We're still outsiders."

I thought for a moment then reached back and took out my wallet. I pulled out a picture of Johny then threw the rest into the bushes. Haley's eyes grew three times as she stared at what I had done.

"We live just north of Elmira," I told her. "We're married. We were visiting your grandmother in ... Twin Falls, you're mother's mother, when the asteroid hit."

"Irene," Haley said, "Irene Frost."

I nodded. Wow, she picked up on things fast.

Her brow furrowed. "But we don't have wedding rings. That's the first thing they will notice."

"We had to trade them for food."

She smiled. "Yes, so sad. Young newlyweds being put through so much. Such a shame."

"Hey," I said. "It's not far from the truth. I wish I had a wedding ring to trade for food or formula."

She reached out and touched my arm then pulled me down so she could kiss my cheek. "Don't worry. We'll make it."

I laughed. That was my job. To be the positive one.

We hurried through the small town and were on the main road west when I realized just how things had changed. Again, one of those epiphany moments. No cars. We were walking for four hours and hadn't seen a moving car. It hadn't sunk in when we were on the river. Not really. Before, I would have been picked up in the first hour. A hundred cops out looking for me. But now? There really wasn't anything they could do about it. If they sent the few guards from the prison. One, where would they look? They didn't have enough people. And by the time they organized a posse, we'd be long gone. Besides. Who would want to join a posse?

We skipped lunch to stretch out our food. Of course, Britney got a bottle. Babies don't understand sacrifice.

Twice we saw people. Once an old man came out of his house to stand on the porch, a shotgun in his arms. Quietly watching us walk by.

The second time, a dog raced out of the trees to greet us, slamming to a halt to sniff at Jordan. A woman in her mid-thirties followed, waving a leash, calling for her dog.

Haley grabbed the dog's collar and held her for the woman.

The woman frowned as she relieved Haley of the dog's collar then scurried off, shuddering as she looked back at me.

"Wow," I said, "People sure are skittish around here."

Haley laughed as she patted my arm. "You just don't realize how intimidating you are. Especially when you scowl."

"I wasn't scowling."

"Ha," Haley barked before she could stop herself. "You are always scowling. Either that or smirking."

I wondered if she was right. Was I that kind of person, pissed off at the world?

As if seeing my discomfort she took my hand and said, "Don't worry. I'm in love with the scowling monster."

Laughing, I shook my head. Who was I to complain, I had the prettiest girl in the world. No complaints on my end.

Later that evening I found a place by the side of a creek and set up the tarp into a tent and spread out our blankets. Once I had a fire going, I grabbed a thin tree branch and started carving a spear.

"What are you going to do with that?" Haley asked.

I nodded to the creek, "Get dinner."

She laughed then stopped herself when she saw I was serious. "They're trout. They won't let you get within a mile of them."

Gritting my teeth I scowled at her and marched off up the creek swearing I wouldn't return until I had enough for dinner.

Haley called out after me, but I ignored her. Don't tell me I couldn't do something, I mumbled to myself as I started looking for a spot. Then almost laughed at myself, what did I know about rushing streams and mountain trout?

Taking a deep breath, I focused on what needed to be done. I wasn't going back empty-handed. Not only did I have to show Haley I could do it. But we needed the food. This wasn't just an ego thing. This was a staying-alive thing.

Chapter Twenty-Seven

Haley

I glanced up the creek where Tanner had gone. Was he okay? The guy hadn't grown up in the woods. But then I laughed at myself. The man was the size of a small mountain. Nothing could hurt him. Words I would learn to regret.

I was wondering if I should start a small pot of rice. We could mix it with tuna fish for protein. When Jordan stood up and looked up the path.

Okay, the man was just too perfect. Walking back into camp holding three trout. Smiling like he'd just conquered the world.

"How?" I gasped.

He shrugged. "It wasn't that hard. You just have to think like a fish."

I scoffed as I quickly relieved him of the fish and started cleaning them. I fed the guts to Jordan then skewered the fish and hung them over the fire.

"You really are amazing," I said to him as I adjusted the fish.

He laughed. "Don't you forget it?"

"Don't go getting a big head. We've got a long way to go. Another fifty miles."

He nodded as he leaned back against a log and let out a long breath. "That's tomorrow. Tonight we eat."

The next morning I woke hugging Britney, Tanner hugging me. All of us buried under layers of blankets. My world filled with rightness.

"Morning, sweetness," he said as he nuzzled my neck.

I sighed and sank back into him, but Britney stirred and whimpered wanting her diaper changed. Sighing, I focused on her while Tanner passed out a couple of crackers for our breakfast. We hit the road twenty minutes after waking up.

I-90 was wide and curved through the mountains. An easy walk. We would look into each car as we passed but they'd been picked clean by fellow travelers long ago. We did find two empty water bottles.

We hit Cour d'Alene just before noon. Tanner hesitated as we drew closer. I frowned at him until I realized he was worried that someone here had gotten word of his escape. Reaching back I took his hand. Silently letting him know we'd face it together. There really wasn't any other way but through the small city.

We needn't have worried. There were no barricades at the city limits. We learned later that the barricades were all at the border with Washington on the other side of the city. Mostly trying to keep the people from Spokane from overwhelming the state. But once you were inside, you were free to go wherever you wanted.

"Food," Tanner said. "We need to find food."

"No," I told him. "it's only three days to my grandfather's farm. Fifteen miles a day. We have enough to last. Don't do anything risky. Not for food."

He studied me for a long moment then nodded. "Okay. Nothing risky. Good. You know me. I never take risks."

I snapped out a quick laugh at him and his silliness. The man was constantly putting himself at risk. Always placing himself between me and danger. I'd seen it countless times, but I honestly believe he wasn't even aware he was doing it.

Cour D'Alene was crowded. People out and about, searching for food would be my guess. I did notice that the clothes seemed to be baggy. As if people had lost weight. Only a couple of weeks into this disaster and it was already showing. What would they look like six months from now?

We were about a mile in when we came across a crowd of about a dozen people gathered around a man with three deer carcasses hanging behind him. A fourth on a table in front. Three men with rifles stood to the side as guards.

The man was butchering the deer and selling the meat. Trading it for gold and jewels. An older woman held out two diamond studs. In the old days. Four thousand dollars worth. Now it got her ten pounds of venison. And she was ecstatic to get it. That was a week's worth of food. I couldn't help but wonder what she would do when she ran out of jewelry.

Tanner hesitated as we passed. I could see him staring at all that red meat and knew he was salivating. Trout was nice. But it wasn't as filling as good red meat. Guys were like that. Anything short of beef was an appetizer.

No police, no soldiers. Wow, just people trying to make it. In the afternoon, a wagon drawn by four horses pulled past us. Five armed men sitting on maybe four hundred sacks of flour, staring at anyone who might think about trying to take it from them.

"Where did they get that?" I asked Tanner.

He shrugged. "A warehouse somewhere. They were smart and got organized. Got a wagon. Got horses. Got men. And went and took it before someone else. Those are the type of people who are going to survive."

"But it's not fair. Having all that food. They should share."

Tanner laughed. "Fair disappeared a couple of weeks ago. Should we share our rice? How about the baby formula? What would Britney have if we gave it all away."

My stomach clenched at the thought. Was Tanner right? Had it become the law of the jungle? Take what you need. No, the world couldn't become that cruel. We couldn't let it slide back into barbarism.

But what could we do to stop it?

A sadness filled me as I began to realize what we had lost. Not the technology. Not all the benefits of a modern world. Not the labor-saving devices or the special things that made life fun. No, we had lost the luxury of excess. Before, there was always enough to go around. You didn't have to worry about your next meal. Enough slack in the system to let people take risks. To let people be different. Enough extra that you didn't have to constantly work for your next meal.

Even the homeless people could get a meal at a soup kitchen or a shelter. No, we had enough so it was easy to be kind. Really, the last couple hundred years had been the first time in history that we had all gotten so far from the source of our food.

That was what civilization was about. Creating enough, more than enough. Freeing up workers from the fields to spend time inventing new things that made life easier. And we'd lost that. My heart soured as I looked at Britney and realized what she would never know.

We hit Highway 95, headed north, and worked our way out of the city and its suburbs before coming to a shuttered amusement park. Tanner froze as he studied, his brow furrowing then he laughed.

"What?" I asked.

"Oh, I was just remembering a zombie movie where they all ended up in an amusement park fighting for their lives. Come on. Let's check it out. Maybe we can crash here."

I could only stare at him. The place reminded him of zombies, and he wanted to stay. Boys were different.

He tore a piece of plywood off a wooden fence and helped me through. It looked like the place had been closed for a couple of years. Rollercoasters beginning to rust. Empty barker game stalls missing their stuffed animals.

Tanner pointed to a snack bar with wooden shutters closing everything off. Raising an eyebrow he smiled then dropped his pack so he could rip a shutter free and step inside.

"Hey," he yelled as he peeked back out holding half a bag of popcorn seeds. Unfortunately, that was all we found. But we were able to get a big pot and cook it up. I missed butter and salt like I missed my family. But it filled out stomachs.

We found an office with a couch and a couple of chairs. We started a fire just outside the door, enough to throw some light into the room but keeping the smoke out. When we woke the next morning Tanner smiled at me. "Another day closer."

"And no zombies," I said to him. "There is always a silver lining. This would have been so much worse with zombies."

"Believe me," Tanner said. "There are enough monsters out there."

I smiled. I had my own monster, so I was okay. I'd put him up against any out there. Oh Haley, if I had only known.

We spent the next night next to a large lake. Tanner was unable to get any trout, so we ended up dipping into our rice and tuna.

The next morning we crossed a long bridge into Sandpoint. "This is the largest city around."

Tanner scoffed and shook his head. "What? Ten thousand people. That's a block in New York."

I laughed. "Yeah, but, when we get to my Papa's we can get stuff to trade. He must have years' worth of food set aside. We can bring some of it back here for Baby formula."

Tanner nodded.

As we drew closer, I began to worry. Things were going too well. Tanner's escape. No one chasing us. Enough food. Surely something would go wrong. The trip had thrown a hundred obstacles in our way. Surely it wasn't done.

No, I told myself. Do not take on unnecessary stress. Surely, we were past the worst of it. No. Positive thoughts, I told myself. Only positive thoughts. I would be seeing my grandfather in a few hours. Maybe we would be there in time for dinner.

Several hours later we'd moved into a forest with small homes every few miles or so. Suddenly Tanner said, "I wonder if any of your family has made it so far."

I hesitated and glanced over at him. "Are you worried about meeting my family?"

He balked then shrugged. "You've got a brother, a cousin, a grandfather, and an uncle. And we … well. We are close. And there's Britney. They're going to jump to conclusions."

My heart melted. The boy was so cute when he was worried. He let it show so rarely that it really was endearing. I reached over and patted his arm. "They will be cool with it as long as you make me an honorable woman. If not. Papa has several shotguns."

I've got to give him credit. He didn't blanch. "No one will have to force me into marrying you."

Hugging his arm I lifted up to kiss him on the cheek before stepping out and leading the way. "Come on. I want to get home so we can start our new life."

He sighed, adjusted the straps to the pack then patted his leg for Jordan to come when a buzz passed my ear followed immediately by a gunshot.

I froze for the briefest of seconds to try and understand what was happening when a thump behind me made my heart shatter. Turning I saw Tanner slumped on the ground, blood leaking from his head.

"NOOOOOOOO!" I yelled as I rushed back to drop next to him. My world ending. No, this was impossible. I couldn't understand. We were so close to home. To safety. No, I couldn't lose him. Britney screamed as I bent over, shaking Tanner, demanding he acknowledge me. Demanding that he live.

"Please," I begged as I put my hand on his chest, praying he would take a breath. Suddenly I was pulled back away from him. Twisting I found a tall man glaring at me with evil eyes then down at Tanner and smiling.

One of the men from Tanner's prison I realized. That large man Tanner told me not to worry about.

"The idiot always did talk too much." The man said. "Always going on about his beautiful, perfect girlfriend and taking her to some farm north of Elmira." Then, still holding my collar, he turned to point his pistol down at Tanner. Getting ready to shoot him again.

"No," I screamed as I shoved my shoulder into his arm. The gun exploded, the bullet landing a foot past Tanner.

"You bitch," he said as he backhanded me across the cheek.

I didn't see stars. I didn't feel pain. All I knew was that I couldn't let this man shoot Tanner. Not again. Reaching up I tried to scratch his face. Anything to pull his attention away from Tanner.

Instead of hitting me again, he lifted me and Britney and started carrying us away. Jordan was barking but the man ignored him. He'd figured out that Jordan wasn't going to attack. It wasn't in his nature.

"You can't," I yelled as I tried to twist out of his grasp. I needed to get back to Tanner. But the man was too strong and with every step I felt my world dissolving. Tanner was dead. There had been too much blood. A sadness filled me as I realized what I had lost. The love of my life.

"No," I cried as a weariness washed over me. Life had no meaning.

I couldn't, I thought. Tanner wouldn't want me to give up. Not like this. Besides, I needed to keep Britney alive, but most of all. I needed to survive long enough to kill this man.

Chapter Twenty-Eight

Tanner

A blackness surrounded me, holding me down. A nothingness that became a ceiling keeping me from something important.

Pushing, I tried to rise up from the blackness, tried to understand what was keeping me down. But nothing worked, nothing made sense.

Slowly, a memory formed. Haley, smiling, walking in front of me. Those delicious hips swinging. Britney babbling about nothing. Jordan wagging his tail. Life. Life was good. But the blackness was keeping me from it.

Without warning, I felt myself being dragged back down into the nothingness and a fear filled me. If I sank into it, I would never come back.

"No," I grumbled and for the first time heard a sound. My voice. It was something to hold onto. Something real as I pushed up through the darkness to open one eye. Oh, the pain. Somebody had hit me upside the head with a sledgehammer and left a construction crew behind to finish the job.

"God, that hurts," I mumbled to myself as I reached up to feel my wound. Sticky blood. I was covered in it. Still sticky, I realized. That meant something but I couldn't figure it out.

Suddenly a new fear filled me. Where was Haley? I was hurt. I knew my girl. She wouldn't have left me like this. She'd have moved heaven and earth to make sure I was okay. But no Haley, No Jordan.

My heart fell as I twisted to try and get my arms under me, but it was too much, too soon, and the blackness returned,

.oOo.

<u>Haley</u>

A numbness filled my soul. Tanner was dead. I saw the blood. His lifeless body lying on the ground.

"This way," the man, Tanner's killer, said as he grabbed my arm and pulled me up a trail. I followed meekly, unable to understand what to do. Tanner was dead. Nothing I did would make any difference.

A sadness like nothing I had ever known washed through me. God, I had loved him so much. He had been so perfect. Oh yes, he had his flaws, Sometimes he was just too much. I couldn't force him to do anything he didn't want to do. And he tended to not see the good in the world. But he had been mine and a more perfect man had never been created.

"No," I mumbled as I fell to my knees and started to cry. A deep ugly cry.

A hand grabbed my arm and pulled me up then dragged me up the trail through the trees until we reached a small campsite. Looking back I could see where a person had sat by this log, feeding a small fire, while watching the road. Waiting for us.

I turned to Tanner's killer and glared. He had waited here. "Why? How?" I demanded.

The man, almost as tall as Tanner, smiled then pushed me down to sit next to a log and waved his pistol at me, reminding me that I was his prisoner.

"Why? How?" I repeated as I called Jordan to join me. I dropped an arm around the dog and pulled him close.

Scoffing, the man shook his head. "Heard he broke out. I knew he'd bring you this way. I didn't think things would work out so good. Him dead, you mine."

The bleakness of my future was overwhelming. Once again, I was reminded about what I had lost. This man could never hurt me as much as he already had.

Suddenly he looked over his shoulder back down the trail and I knew he was thinking about going back and shooting Tanner again. I could see the worry in his eyes. He knew how dangerous an angry Tanner could be. But a part of me wanted him to go. Britney and I would escape. And it wasn't as if he could kill Tanner any more than he already had.

But instead, he turned back to me and sneered. Not a smile, not a smirk. An evil sneer. Like I was gunk on his shoe. As I watched, a thousand thoughts floated through his brain. Each one more evil than the next. All dealing with what he was going to do to me.

The sneer shifted over to a smile as he sat down and stared at me. Suddenly I understood. For him, it was the pain he enjoyed inflicting. The anticipation of the pain he would cause drove him. He wanted to see me cry, to beg for my life. He wanted me to know what was going to happen then drag it out for as long as possible before he followed through.

And then he would repeat it, over and over until I was dead.

A gut-wrenching sickness filled me as I saw it all laid out before me.

.oOo.

Tanner

It was easier the second time to pull myself up out of the darkness. Haley. She was my guiding light. She needed me. Every part of me knew she needed me.

This time, when I got my arms underneath me, I pushed up to my knees and waited until the dizziness slacked off before trying to stand.

It was like getting hit by a giant wave, almost knocking me off my feet. I fought the threatening faintness, fought to stay on my feet, terrified the darkness would come back.

"Haley," I whispered to myself as I took my first step. It was like trying to work through Jello. I'd been knocked out before. Anyone doing MMA for any time is going to get it at some point. But this was different. This was a constant pounding in my head. A thousand jackhammers all out competing with each other to see who could drive me crazy first.

Stumbling forward I tried to understand. I was in the middle of a road. We had been walking up the road to Haley's Papa's. Had she gone there?

A pool of blood where I had been hit but no others. She hadn't been wounded. She and the baby were okay. Or at least had been. A burning need filled me, pushing the constant darkness back. An anger like nothing I had ever known filled me. A burning need to kill whatever had taken her from me.

Suddenly, A new fear filled me. What if she had been taken south? I might never find her. How long had I been out? She could be halfway to Seattle by now.

No, suddenly the sticky blood made sense. I hadn't been out too long. Minutes. I was about to call out to her when I saw a footprint on a trail leading up into the trees.

Haley

Suddenly, the look in his eyes shifted over to a lust that made my skin crawl. It was as if he'd become a feral animal. Interested in only one thing. "No," I said as I scooted away.

He laughed and waved his pistol at me, "Put the baby over there. We can do this easy or hard. I just spent six months in jail. But I'll be nice, and let you do easy."

I froze, too terrified to move. All my anger and numbness had disappeared as I saw what was coming. Keep Britney alive, I mumbled to myself.

Suddenly, he pushed himself up and took a step towards me. This was it. I couldn't run. Not with Britney. He'd shoot me, leaving her alone to die a slow death. A resignation slowly filled me. I was trapped. But deep down, I knew I would keep an eye out for an opportunity, a chance to stick a knife into his ribs or smash his head with a rock.

Somewhere I would get a chance.

He reached down for me, Pushing me onto my back.

.oOo.

Tanner

It took every effort to make my way up the trail. Twice I saw what I assumed was Haley's footprint. Next to a man's a big print.

He had her, I realized. He'd shot me, then taken her and the baby.

A new fear filled me. There was only one reason to kill me and take her. Suddenly Jordan barked up ahead. An angry bark. Using the trees, I pulled myself up the trail as fast as I could to find Miller bent over Haley, fumbling at her clothes.

I didn't think, I just charged.

Miller suddenly looked over his shoulder at me rushing towards him. For the briefest moment, his eyes grew three sizes in shock, but he shifted quickly and lifted his pistol, shooting twice before I crashed into him.

At that point there really was no doubt as to how things would work out. I had his pistol hand in one grip, keeping the weapon away from me or Haley. The other hand had him by the throat.

He brought his knee up into my crotch then rolled away from me. I reacted like I'd been trained and rolled with him, knocking the gun from his hand then putting him in a headlock and squeezing with everything I had.

The darkness was threatening to return as I tried to focus. Really, it would be a fight as to who would pass out first.

Slowly the lights were going out in his eyes when his hand reached through the pine needles and found his pistol. He was bringing it up to shoot me when I did the only thing I could. I twisted and broke his neck.

He slumped down, dead.

"Tanner," Haley gasped as she rushed to me. "You're alive."

I smiled at her, then passed out.

.oOo.

Haley

He was alive. My Tanner was alive. It was impossible to believe. Somehow, he had survived. Somehow he had saved me again.

"No," I begged as I saw him slump. Rushing I got behind him, stopping his head from hitting the ground. He was out.

Swallowing hard, I glanced over at my attacker and felt nothing. Tanner had killed him. Good. The man deserved to die.

Tanner moaned in his sleep, forcing me to focus on what was important. "Stay here," I said needlessly then rushed down the trail to get our backpack from the middle of the road. When I got back to Tanner he hadn't moved.

"I've got to use one of your diapers," I said to Britney as I removed a cloth diaper and started to wipe at his head. I was able to wipe

311

enough away to see where the bullet had gouged out a six-inch strip of his scalp above his left ear. Exposing the white bone of his skull.

My stomach clenched when I saw it, but I pushed my fears away and tore a second diaper to make a bandage.

After that, I used one of our blankets for a pillow and covered him in the others. Then I dragged our attacker twenty feet away. Enough to where I didn't have to look at him. I got Britney fed, Cooked some rice, then made a broth with the tuna and waited.

It was after dark before he woke up. Mumbling something about rivers.

"Tanner," I whispered getting up on my knees to kneel next to him.

He smiled faintly then closed his eyes.

"No," I snapped. "No, don't leave me," I said more softly.

"I will never leave you," he whispered, and I knew it was true. He would make it. He would get me to my Papa's. after that. We would have a whole life together.

Chapter Twenty-Nine

Haley

We walked up the dirt road to my Papa's. Storm, the horse he kept just for Cassie and me raced across the field towards us.

My stomach fluttered when I saw the farmhouse. The tree house and swing. Everything was just like I remembered it.

I shifted Britney in my arms and reached over to hold Tanner's hand.

As we drew closer, a man stood up on the porch and stared at us.

"Ryan?" I called as my heart soared.

"Haley?" He said as he jumped down and rushed towards us, limping. I noticed a half dozen other people came out of the house, but all I could do was hug Ryan. My family. A part of my family had survived.

"You made it," he said. "I thought you would have it the hardest, coming from New York." He then looked up at Tanner. I had to smile. Ryan was a big guy, but he wasn't in Tanner's league.

"This is Tanner," I said as I laid a hand on Tanner's shoulder. "My fiancé." Tanner didn't flinch he just held out his hand for Ryan as if he was introduced as a woman's fiancé every day. I swear the man knew what was important.

Ryan shook his hand then glanced down at the baby and raised an eyebrow.

"I'll explain. Where's Papa?"

Ryan frowned, stared down at the ground before saying. "He's dead. Squatters killed him then tried to take this place. I killed them and took it back."

Tanner nodded and I could see the respect in his eyes.

My heart broke. I had so hoped to see my grandfather again. He would know what to do. In any situation, you could always rely on him to figure it out. Plus, I had wanted to introduce him to Tanner. They were so alike, tough, no nonsense type people. I knew they would have liked each other.

A sadness filled me. But something was different about me. Something new. A few weeks ago, I would have been devastated. Now, I was hurt, sad, but I knew we could get past this, we had gotten across the continent. We could handle anything.

Smiling, I handed Britney to Tanner so I could slip my arm into Ryan's. It felt so good. So right to be home with family. "Cassie? Chase? Your dad?" I asked.

Ryan shook his head. "Not yet. But it's still early. And they're trying to keep people out of Idaho."

Tanner scoffed. "You're telling me."

"They will make it," I said. "Chase will come waltzing in here all alone, wondering what the fuss is all about. And Cassie, you know her. Nothing will stop her."

Ryan nodded as he glanced over his shoulder, south, looking for his sister.

Suddenly we were surrounded by a half dozen strangers. One boy, three girls, and two older women. I lifted an eyebrow at Ryan.

He smiled as he slipped an arm around a pretty brunette and said, "It's a long story. I'm sure it is just like yours. Full of monsters and mayhem."

I laughed as I took the baby back from Tanner then said to my cousin. "It's not a big deal when you have your own pet monster."

Epilogue

Tanner

I stood up and pushed at my lower back. It was different I thought with a smile. Digging in the ground for yourself and your family. Taking a moment, I looked out over the field. Everyone except Britney was digging, either in the field or one of the four gardens.

We were so lucky, I thought to myself. The old man had seed potatoes. Corn, things we would need to get through next winter. The food he'd put up last year would help us get through until we could harvest from the forest. It had already proven invaluable as trade goods. Six quart jars of tomato sauce and three of green beans for one large can of powdered baby formula.

It would get us through another month. Two more and we could start to wean Britney.

We'd converted the tack room in the barn for the three of us. Ryan was talking about adding on to the main house, but I wanted to build a cabin off to the side. I like Haley and I having our own privacy.

Sighing, I wiped at my forehead then returned to digging. These potatoes weren't going to plant themselves.

Suddenly, Jordan barked, facing the road. I lifted my hand to shade my eyes and saw a boy, maybe ten, racing down the road towards us. I turned to make sure young Paul was still digging next to his sister.

I immediately looked beyond this new boy as my hand dropped to the gun on my hip. Neither Ryan nor I went anywhere without a gun.

The boy saw me and slid through the split rail fence and rushed up to me. "Chester Conrad? I need to talk to Chester Conrad."

"He's dead," I said, pointing to the grave on the other side of the barn.

The boy looked around, obviously terrified, then pulled himself together. "Ryan, Cassie, Haley?

"Hey Ryan," I called to Haley's cousin who was already walking towards us.

The kid asked him, "Are you Ryan Conrad."

Ryan nodded.

The kid slumped with relief. "Chase, your cousin, needs your help. He sent me to get you. He said to bring your guns.

The End

Author's Afterword

I do hope you enjoyed the novel. My last series explored what happens when everyone dies, and technology is lost. This time, I wanted to explore what happens when Technology is lost resulting in everyone dying. Again, the important question, what would I do in that situation.

I have often wondered what would happen if my family was separated by great distance when the world ended?

As always, I wish to thank friends who have helped, authors Erin Scott, and Anya Monroe. And my special friend Sheryl Turner. But most of all I want to thank my wife Shelley for all she puts up with. It can be difficult being an author's spouse. We have a tendency to live in our own little worlds. Our minds drifting to strange new places, keeping us unaware of what is happening around us. Thankfully I am married to a woman who knows when to let me write and knows when to pull me back into the real world.

The first book in the series Impact (The End of Times 1) is available on Amazon. I hope to have the next book in the series, "Survivors", out in a few months. In the mean time, I have put in a small sample of the first book in my other series, The End of Everything (The End of Everything 1) truly believe you would enjoy it.

Thank you again

Nate Johnson

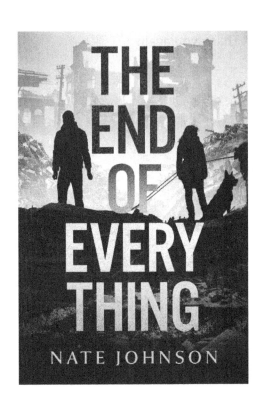

The End of Everything

Chapter One

Nick

I didn't say goodbye to my mom that day. A fact that I would regret on my deathbed. Being an angry seventeen-year-old was my only excuse. It was my mom who sent me away. Her way of stopping me from becoming an even worse jerk.

A boy gets in one fight and the world comes crashing down on him. Granted, breaking a guy's arm and knocking out a couple of teeth for the other one made it seem worse. But then they had it coming, believe me.

Anyway, Mom figured six weeks as a Counselor in Training at Camp Tecumseh in Eastern Pennsylvania would keep me away from bad influences. A nice peaceful summer she said. God, how wrong could a person be?

But like I said, I didn't even turn to look at her when I stepped up onto the bus. If I'd known I'd never see her again, I might have given a damn. I might not have been such a jerk. At least I like to think so. It's how I keep from beating myself up about it.

I nodded to the driver. The same guy I remembered from my camp five years earlier.

Then Dad died and going away to summer camp became an unnecessary expense. But Mom thought it would be good for me to do this CIT thing. It didn't cost anything. Free labor. So here I was on a bus to hell.

It was a day before the camp was supposed to start so this was just for the early birds. The kids and CITs that couldn't show up tomorrow. Nine kids and two girl CITs. Tomorrow there would be a hundred and forty campers arriving along with twenty CITs and staff.

Being the typical boy, I checked out the girls immediately. Both about my age, maybe sixteen. The one on the right had long brown hair in a ponytail. Pretty, with discerning eyes. Something told me, rich girl. I don't know. Maybe it was just the attitude.

The one on the left. Shorter, blond, with glasses. Pretty but not as much as ponytail.

I knew what they saw when they looked back at me. A tall guy with a scowl. I had a habit of standing out in a crowd. A fact that always bugged me at my core. I wasn't lanky. More solid. But tall. Six three and I wouldn't see eighteen for another two months.

The rest of the bus had nine kids, eleven to twelve years old, spread out. Five girls and four boys. They were looking at me with shaded frowns. Was I the typical jerk or a special one?

Shifting my backpack on my shoulder, I made my way down the aisle to the end then jerked my thumb for the kid in the back seat to move.

The kid had the good sense to scurry out of the seat.

I plopped down and stared into nothing.

The driver pushed the bus into gear, and we were off. Six weeks I thought. I could do anything for six weeks. It wasn't the end of the world.

Ha, that always makes me laugh. When it comes to being mistaken. No person had ever been more wrong.

The bus crawled through the small town and then started up a switch-back two-lane road into the mountains. I stared out the window at the forest and occasional farm of the Pocono Mountains. Not much different than the area around Syracuse, I thought.

Six weeks I reminded myself. I guess it was better than jail, even if only slightly.

A little over an hour and we finally got there, about twenty-five miles out from the town. I guess this place was farther out than I remembered. When you are a little kid, you don't pick up on things like that. But we were finally there, and things hadn't changed one bit.

About twenty cabins clustered on the far end of the lake. Four main buildings up on a hill above the lake and cabins. On the left, the admin building. Built of thick logs. Next, the combined mess hall and kitchen. Then the showers and restrooms. If I remembered correctly divided down the middle with six showers and eight cubicles on each side. It got busy in the morning, to say the least. And finally, the staff building. More like a dormitory.

Everything was as I remembered it. Even the same float sat in the middle of the lake.

I almost smiled to myself when I remembered the first time, I had swum all the way out there in a race with Billy Jenkins. I wondered where he was. Probably hanging out with his friends, playing video games, or a pick-up basketball game. Things I would end up never knowing. Billy was lost to history. As if he never lived.

I wonder if he'd been playing video games when it all ended. Fighting off monsters while invisible ones ate him up from the inside.

Three sailboats were moored to a pier sticking out into the lake, their sails furled and stowed. The large firepit off to the side looked like it was all ready for hotdogs and smores.

It was the first warm day of summer late spring day. A little cooler up here in the mountains with a high blue sky. But it was the smell though that told me I was somewhere different. A green smell filled with life. Or maybe it was the absence of car exhaust and wet asphalt. Anyway, I took a deep breath and almost relaxed. Then I remembered I was angry at the world and pushed it aside.

The blond and ponytail were waiting for me. The driver Thompson or Thomas or something was rounding up the kids and said he'd be back for us in a minute. The blond stepped forward with a wide smile and I knew the type immediately. She would want to be friends. For life even.

"I'm Brie Osborn," she said holding out her hand.

I shook it, making sure not to apply too much pressure. Mom had gone out of her way to try and make a gentleman out of me. For the most part, she had failed, but some things stuck.

"And this is Jenny," she said indicating the pony-haired girl.

"Jennifer," the girl corrected as she held out her hand.

Again, I made a point of not squeezing too hard. For the briefest moment we stared into each other's eyes, and I saw it immediately. She didn't like me. To her, I was a bug that had dropped onto her plate of food.

I don't know what I'd done. And really, it didn't matter. She wouldn't be the first pretty girl who didn't think I was worth a damn.

Letting go of her hand, I turned away to look out over the camp. Six weeks, I reminded myself and then I was out of here. Two groups of snot-nosed kids to be shepherded.

As I stood there, an awkward silence fell over the three of us. I wanted to smile. They were pretty girls and weren't used to being ignored. But no way was I getting interested. Well, at least not officially.

Thankfully the awkward silence was broken by Thompson returning. He was the manager, I reminded myself. He'd been running this place for years. He had everything down to a system if I remembered correctly. A tight timetable that kept everyone too busy to get into trouble.

I wondered if he knew about me. There had been a police report. But the charges had been dropped when they finally figured out the two other guys were even worse jerks than me. No. He didn't I realized. He would never have accepted Mom's application.

Oh, well. No need to inform him of my past. I'd do my time then go home to finish out my senior year and then off to start some kind of life that I still hadn't figured out.

That memory. Standing there, thinking about the future hurts now. More than you will ever know.

Thompson returned after showing the kids their cabin. He had to be in his late forties with a bit of a paunch. A gray sweatshirt with Camp Tecumseh across the chest and a Yankee's ball cap that looked like it had been dunked in the lake a dozen times.

"Make sure they feel comfortable. Stop the arguments over who gets which bunk. You know stuff like that. Then have them up at the mess hall by five."

Jenny frowned at him. I had determined that I would refer to her as Jenny just to piss her off. "Aren't there any counselors? I thought we were supposed to be learning. You know the whole 'in training' part of things."

The old man had a brief worried look then shook his head. "A couple of them were supposed to show up today. But they got delayed. They'll be here tomorrow along with the rest."

Jenny decided not to push the issue but picked up her backpack and started down the hill. Obviously, she knew where she was going. If I had to guess, I bet she'd been a camper here for ten years and was going through this CIT stuff so she could get on staff next year.

As she walked down the hill, I had to admit her butt was way above average in jeans that were just the right amount of tight.

Thompson caught me checking her out and shook his head before slapping my shoulder. "Don't even think about it."

I laughed for the first time in two weeks. That was going to be an impossibility. I was a seventeen-year-old boy. That was all I thought about.

The blond, Brie, I reminded myself, hurried to catch up with her friend.

Old man Thompson showed me the boy's CIT cabin. On the opposite side of the camp from the girl's CIT cabin. With eighteen cabins for the campers between them. Obviously, these people weren't stupid.

I threw my stuff onto the farthest of eight bunks and wondered what the other CITs would be like. I shrugged my shoulders. I wasn't here to make lifetime friends.

Okay, it couldn't be avoided any longer. I found the cabin with the four boys and entered without knocking. You would have thought that a werewolf had stepped into the place. All four froze, looking at me with wide eyes.

I could see it instantly. Like all boys. At some point in their life they had been bullied by older, bigger boys. The natural instinct was to freeze in the presence of a predator.

Scanning them I saw the usual. Kids. The smallest in the back frowned, but I had to give him credit, he didn't look away.

"I'm Nick," I told them. "I'm supposed to make sure you guys don't get lost on the way to the mess hall. Any problems I need to solve? ... Good. Finish up."

They scrambled to make up their bunks. Sheets and blankets had been left on each one. Once that was done I had them put their stuff away in lockers. They still had that haunted look, waiting for things to go wrong.

"God, lighten up guys," I said. "I won't screw with you. Not unless you deserve it. What are your names?"

"Mike," a chunky kid with red hair said then bit his tongue, obviously wondering if that was the right answer. "Mike Jackson."

Okay. I know I can be intimidating. My size, the fresh scar over my left eyebrow. Oh yeah, and the permanent scowl.

"Carl, Carl Bender," a lanky black kid. Okay, if we had a basketball tournament, I was picking him for my team.

"Anthony, but I prefer Tony. Tony Gallo," A dark-haired Italian kid said as he pushed his glasses back up to the bridge of his nose.

I nodded then turned to the last one. The smallest, and probably youngest. "And you."

The kids finished putting his stuff away, hesitated, then said "Patterson Abercrombie."

The other boys laughed, and I saw the pain shoot behind the kid's eyes. I wondered how many times that had happened in his life and how many times it would in the future. Of course, we all ended up having way worse futures than people laughing at our names. But I didn't know that then so I did what anyone would have done and laughed along with everyone else, but I followed it up by saying, "That's too hard to remember. Besides, a name like that makes you sound like a stockbroker, and you look too intelligent to ever fall into that scam. So I'm going to call you … Bud. That okay?"

The kid's eyes grew big, and I knew he'd never had a nickname in his entire life. At least not one he liked. Smiling, he nodded.

"Okay," I said as I examined them. "Mike, Carl, Tony, and Bud. God, it sounds like a boy band. You guys break out singing and I'll disown you. I swear."

They laughed and the tension was broken. I wasn't a special jerk, perhaps only a regular one and they could live with that.

Oh, if we had but known what a person could live with and without.

Chapter Two

Jenifer

Camp Tecumseh, God, I loved it. The one place in the world that was safe. Safe from overprotective parents and a judgmental world. No maids reporting to mom every time I broke the slightest rule. I swear I think she paid them extra for every time they ratted me out. Here I could be me. Jennifer O'Brien.

The smells, the colors, the soft breeze. All of it brought back fond memories. And now, finally, I was a CIT. Everything was how it was supposed to be. CIT this summer. Then senior at school next year. After that, either Harvard or Yale. My parents were still arguing about which. But none of that mattered. I was at Camp Tecumseh for the next six weeks and my future was bright.

HA! What a crock of ... stuff that turned out to be.

When we reached the CIT cabin I turned and looked back at that boy going into his cabin. Well, nothing could be perfect. All I could do was shake my head. This Nick person was so wrong for Camp Tecumseh.

I knew the type only too well. A bad boy to his very core. It was obvious, the heavy scowl, the wide shoulders, denim jacket, and the way he talked. As if everyone else in the world was without value. Yes, A definite bad boy.

Unlike most other girls. Bad boys did nothing for me. No fluttering butterflies. No halted breath. No, they were a waste with no socially redeeming value. Especially here.

Deep down, I knew the problem was that he reminded me of my dad. That same cocky attitude and that inability to be faithful. Mom might forgive my dad, but I still couldn't.

Brie glanced to where I was looking and smiled. "It is going to be an interesting summer."

I laughed and shook my head. "Let's hope not. Don't forget. We are here to keep the peace and make sure nothing bad happens."

Well, we failed at that, didn't we? Or at least the world did.

After Brie and I got settled we headed over to the girl's cabin. Brie and I had known each other for eight years. Not bosom buddies. But we'd shared a cabin a couple of times. Been on the same tug-a-war teams that type of thing.

When we got to the girl's cabin we knocked and waited to be let in. Five young girls. Three of them had been here before. The other two were newbies, watching the others to see what to do next.

I was pleased to see bunks being made and things put away in lockers. Eleven and twelve year old's. God, I remembered that awful time of being in between. No longer child, not yet woman. I smiled to myself. It was why girls this age formed such tight bonds with each other. They were the only ones who truly understood.

"I'm Jennifer, this is Brie. We're here if you need any help. Answer any questions."

The five girls stared back, some shrugging before returning to finish their work. I couldn't help but smile. Brie and I were already outsiders. We might be used for information, but we weren't one of them.

An hour on a bus and a shared cabin and they were already forming a team to face the world. After introductions, I watched them for a moment and immediately started putting them into categories.

Ashley Chan, Asian-American. A quick smile and a born helper. She was already assisting Katy Price in finishing with her bunk.

Katy Price, brunet, shy. When I saw her slip a Harry Potter book into her locker I had to smile. Only a true bookworm brings a book to camp. I knew she would have preferred to lay in the shade of a tree and read instead of swimming or games. No, for her, other worlds were her fascination.

Then there was Nicole Parsons. She was easy to figure out. A hint of eyeshadow and lip gloss. Twelve going on sixteen. With a hint of toughness behind her eyes. Nicole was the type of person you didn't want to get on the wrong side of.

Emma Davis, a strawberry blond was watching everyone else with a keen eye. A newbie, she had a natural curiosity. The diary sitting on top of her upper bunk confirmed it. She'd chronicle every detail. Locking onto paper what she couldn't remember.

And finally, Harper Reed. The other first-timer. Confident, not needing to watch the others to know what to do. Tall, pretty on her way to being beautiful. A future heartbreaker. Supermodel in training. A sketchbook slipped under her mattress exposed the secret to her soul. An artist. I wondered if she was any good. Yes, I thought. There was something about Harper that said she would be good at anything she did.

Five young girls. My responsibility. At least until the counselors showed up.

I shook my head. They really should have been here already, getting ready. I was disappointed in them. It was just plain wrong to treat Camp as unimportant. Of course, now it is hard to blame people for being late when they were in the process of dying. It seems sort of petty, if you know what I mean.

After getting everyone settled, we headed up to the mess hall for dinner. The seven of us went through the line for salad, garlic bread, and spaghetti. Not my favorite, but that was the thing about Camp food. You ate what they served, or you went without.

We all sat at a table off to the right. Talking, sharing, an occasional giggle. When the boys showed up, the feeling in the room changed. I couldn't help but shake my head. Even at this young age, the girls were very aware of boys being in the vicinity.

Of course the male members of our species were typical, loud, and rambunctious, with someone throwing a punch at another's shoulder. It was almost as if they were trying to draw attention to themselves. The four of them got their meals and made it a point of sitting as far away as possible.

They wanted attention but didn't want to get contaminated by girls.

Then there was that Nick person. God, what a cold, non-caring, waste of oxygen. He stepped up and Mrs. Smith, the cook, smiled at him as if he were special then gave him a double serving without him having to ask. And of course he skipped the salad entirely.

But it was when he sat down all alone, separate from the boys that I saw his true self. A loner. Most definitely not Camp Tecumseh material. Oh, well, it was only six weeks.

Again, HA!

The next morning was pretty much the same thing only pancakes instead of spaghetti. It had been a restless night. The newness was already wearing off. The girls had probably stayed up half the night sharing stories about where they were from. Now it was simply a matter of waiting for the other campers to show up so we could get started.

I was trying to organize a volleyball game when Mr. Thompson and Mrs. Smith stepped out of the admin building and called, Brie, myself, and Nick over. The camp manager had a deep frown and kept looking to the front gate. Mrs. Smith simply shook her head.

My stomach clenched up just a bit. I knew that look. It was the look my father got when things didn't go the way he expected. It was just a matter of figuring out who to blame.

"There seems to be a problem," he said with a shake of his head.

The three of us stood there waiting. This could be anything from rat poison in the pancake batter to someone forgetting to order enough toilet paper.

I couldn't help but notice that the Nick person didn't frown. I swear the man could have been told he was to die in an hour, and he wouldn't have cared one way or the other.

"It seems," Mr. Thompson continued. "That some of the staff are still delayed. Mrs. Smith will have to drive the other bus."

It was a little confusing, how did he know they weren't arriving. I knew from long experience that there was no cell coverage up here. Then I suddenly realized that as a result of the changes he meant that there weren't going to be any adults left.

"You guys will have to keep an eye on things."

Okay, I could live with that. A bit better than rat poison.

"Nick, you'll be in charge. Keep them away from the lake and the forest. It will only be a couple of hours."

Mr. Bad boy nodded, as if it was no big deal, being left in charge. I of course wanted to scream, how come he got picked? But I had learned long ago not to challenge older men. It was a waste of time, they never saw reason. My father being a prime example.

"There is stuff to make sandwiches," Mrs. Smith said, "If we're not back in time for lunch. But no using the stove and stay out of the ice cream. That is for special circumstances."

That last line makes me want to both laugh and cry. I'll tell you about it when we get to that part of the story.

Mr. Thompson stared at the front gate for a minute and shook his head Then took a deep breath and nodded for Mrs. Smith to follow him.

We three CITs were joined by the nine campers and stood there to watch the two big yellow buses drive through the front gate.

I think that is the point where my story started. Really. There was my life before and my life after. A life in what used to be the normal world and this life. Believe me, they aren't the same. Not even close.

Made in the USA
Coppell, TX
26 November 2024